VILLAGE OF THE MERMAIDS

CARLTON MELLICK III

ERASERHEAD PRESS
PORTLAND, OREGON

ERASERHEAD PRESS
205 NE BRYANT
PORTLAND, OR 97211

WWW.ERASERHEADPRESS.COM

ISBN: 1-62105-088-2

Printed in the USA.

Praise for
Carlton Mellick III

Also by Carlton Mellick III

Satan Burger
Electric Jesus Corpse
Sunset With a Beard (stories)
Razor Wire Pubic Hair
Teeth and Tongue Landscape
The Steel Breakfast Era
The Baby Jesus Butt Plug
Fishy-fleshed
The Menstruating Mall
Ocean of Lard (with Kevin L. Donihe)
Punk Land
Sex and Death in Television Town
Sea of the Patchwork Cats
The Haunted Vagina
Cancer-cute (Avant Punk Army Exclusive)
War Slut
Sausagey Santa
Ugly Heaven
Adolf in Wonderland
Ultra Fuckers
Cybernetrix
The Egg Man
Apeshit
The Faggiest Vampire
The Cannibals of Candyland
Warrior Wolf Women of the Wasteland
The Kobold Wizard's Dildo of Enlightenment +2
Zombies and Shit
Crab Town
The Morbidly Obese Ninja
Barbarian Beast Bitches of the Badlands
Fantastic Orgy (stories)
I Knocked Up Satan's Daughter
Armadillo Fists
The Handsome Squirm
Tumor Fruit
Kill Ball
Cuddly Holocaust
Hammer Wives

AUTHOR'S NOTE

I don't want to sound like a queer or nothing, but I think mermaids are kickass.

Actually, that line from the movie Orgazmo was *unicorns* not *mermaids*, but it might as well have been. Mermaids are kickass, too. In fact, I've always been a huge fan of all the "girly" fantasy creatures: mermaids, fairies, pixies, unicorns, kitty cats with angel wings, and so forth. Maybe it was because I spent way too much time with my little sister when I was a kid. I'd watch all her girly cartoons like Gem or Rainbow Brite and she'd watch my manly cartoons like He-man and G.I. Joe. Maybe that's why we both ended up with interests that were a combination of girly and manly. We'd play games where she was a kickass fairy with swords and machine gun arms and I was a unicorn with tattoos and a chainsaw for a horn. We'd fight bad guys and then go shopping for fashionable new outfits at the imaginary mall.

Those interests kind of never went away for me. Everything I write I try to infuse with a mixture of girly and manly. If I write about tanks I want the tanks to be pink. If I write about mermaids I want them to be vicious and deadly.

I've always loved reinventing traditional fantasy creatures. That was the whole reason I wrote *Warrior Wolf Women of the Wasteland*. It was meant to be my take on werewolves. *Village of the Mermaids* is my take on mermaids. They are not the Disney variety of mermaids. They are feral creatures that want to rip your throat out. That's how mermaids always should be: like the Alien Queen, only cuter.

Village of the Mermaids is my 40th book to be published. It's kind of nuts when I think about it. 40 seems like a hell of a lot of books to have out. But I've been a fulltime writer for about 10 years now. With no day job to get in my way it was kind of easy to write 40 books during that time, especially when the bulk of them are 40,000 words or less.

I've made a commitment to write 4 books a year from now on, one per season. I've been doing that for a while anyway, but now I've decided to make it official. Expect a new book every January, April, July, and October. And the occasional bonus book on special occasions.

At the beginning of this book, there is a bonus deleted scene. It's one of my favorite scenes in the book but it just didn't fit anywhere in the story so it had to be cut. It actually works as a kind of prologue for the book because it takes place before the story begins. But keep in mind that it is no longer meant to be a part of this story. It is non-canon. You might even want to read it a couple of days before you start the book so it feels more like a stand-alone prequel story.

So here it is. Book #40. And it's about mermaids. How awesome is that?

—Carlton Mellick III 3/19/2013 7:51am

FATHER-DAUGHTER TALK
DELETED PREQUEL SCENE

"I'm sure you're wondering why I've called you here today," said Doctor Black, as the smiling little girl entered his office. "Please, take a seat."

He gestured to the small metal chair in the center of the room. She nodded twice and quietly seated herself.

"Back straight," said the doctor, pointing at her abhorrent posture. She straightened her back and raised her chin. It was a drill she knew very well.

Doctor Black stood from his desk and towered above the girl. Her glossy brown eyes twinkled up at him, smiling a chubby smile and fidgeting with a purple-checkered bow in her hair.

"Normally, I would have my secretary inform my colleagues and acquaintances of this information," said the doctor. "But as your father, I decided it might be more appropriate to deliver the news to you personally."

The little girl just smiled at her father, excited to be in the same room with him. Even though they lived together, she hardly ever got to see him in person. He did not take weekends or holidays off. And when she did see him, he rarely spoke to her directly. He was always so busy with his work.

"I called you here to inform you that I have only a week to live," said Doctor Black.

The girl's smile fell from her face. At first, she thought he was joking, but that couldn't be possible. Her father never, ever joked.

"You mean… you're going to die?" she asked, her breath quickening, her eyes moist.

"Correct," said the doctor. "Your mother and I decided it would be best if you were unaware that my disease was terminal until I was in my final days."

The girl stood from her seat and raised her arms up to him, wanting him to hold her, but the doctor wouldn't allow it. He held out his hand so she couldn't come near.

"Hugging is not permitted," he said, and told her to return to her seat.

The girl wiped at her tears.

"So, we'll only be together for another week?" she asked.

The doctor shook his head.

"No," he said. "Unfortunately, I have business to attend to for the rest of the week. I'll be leaving for the airport after this meeting."

The girl's eyes turned bright red until she burst into a crying fit.

"Please, compose yourself," the doctor said, pointing to a strategically placed box of tissues. "This is a place of business."

The girl pulled tissues from the box. She tried to calm herself but was hiccupping with distress.

The doctor looked at his watch. "I've only allotted ten minutes for us to spend together and we've already wasted five, so we should hurry this along."

The doctor handed the girl a pile of envelopes.

"Here are your birthday cards for the next twenty years," said the doctor. "Each contains a hundred dollar bill. Please refrain from opening more than one card per year even if you require the money."

The girl looked at the envelopes. Each one had a different year written on the front. The handwriting was not her father's.

"And here is a list of acceptable career options," said the doctor, handing her a laminated sheet of manila paper. The girl held it like a restaurant menu. "Choose one of them by the time you come of age. I recommend Data Systems Analyst. It is an exciting field that is always in demand."

The girl had a distant look in her eyes. She wasn't even listening to him anymore as he retrieved a stack of DVDs and placed them one by one in her lap.

"This DVD contains my speech that I prepared for your wedding reception," said Doctor Black. "You'll need to find a projector and a good PA system. It might be a little quiet so make sure the volume is adjustable." He pointed at another DVD. "And this one is a congratulatory message for when you have your first son. You might want to watch this one in advance because I discuss suitable names for the child." The girl cradled the DVDs in her arms, embracing his residual warmth. "The rest of the videos are disciplinary lectures if you ever happen to commit a felony, drop out of school, or find yourself inappropriately attracted to members of the same gender."

The girl put the DVDs aside and raised her hands, begging to be hugged.

The doctor just shook his head at her. "I already told you, hugging is not permitted." He pointed at a doll in the corner of the room. "If you must hug something use the hugging dad."

The doll was a life-sized plushy replica of Doctor Black. Its arms were raised in the hugging position, its face drawn with magic marker. Even the doll version of him did not have a smile.

The girl looked at it for a moment, but she did not hug the thing.

"I believe that covers everything," said the doctor. "Do you have any questions?"

The girl trembled in a panic. She could not believe she would never see her father again.

"So I'll never see you again?"

"That is correct."

"It's just me and mommy now?"

"No, I'm afraid not. Unfortunately, your mother was killed in a car accident on the way to work this morning. You will be staying with my secretary's family until your uncle is released from prison next month."

The girl stopped breathing, her eyes shaking at her father. Then she screamed at the top of her lungs.

"I understand this news might also be a bit upsetting to

you, but please compose yourself." Doctor Black pointed at the doll version of himself. "Use the hugging dad."

The girl looked at the doll. Tears poured down her cringing red face.

"I insist," said the doctor. "Whenever you're lonely or upset, just use the hugging dad. I asked my secretary to bring it home with you."

The girl went to the massive doll and awkwardly placed her arms around it, wetting the fabric with her tears.

"Now, if you'll excuse me," said the doctor. "I have a plane to catch."

He straightened his suit and raised his hand. It looked more like he was giving an oath than waving goodbye.

"It has been a pleasure being your father," he said.

Before he could leave his office, the daughter tore away from the dad-shaped doll and attacked the doctor, wrapping her arms around him with all her strength, crying into his lower stomach. The doctor did not hug her back, raising his arms away from her, standing there uncomfortably with the girl coiled around his waist.

"Just for a minute…" the doctor said, attempting to tolerate his daughter's grasp.

He looked at his wristwatch and then let out a loud sigh as the girl created a head-shaped indentation in his abdomen.

VILLAGE OF THE MERMAIDS

CHAPTER ONE
THE MONOCHROME PEOPLE

Doctor Black had the disease. The one nobody liked to talk about.

Everyone on the boat could tell he was infected. No matter how many layers of clothing he wore to conceal his inhuman flesh, they all knew exactly what was wrong with him. And they stayed as far away as they could, crowding into the front half of the ship as if huddled together for warmth.

Only one woman dared approach him—a college-aged girl with short blond hair and a smile too small for her face.

"They say you have Zimmer's Disease," she said to him.

It was not the way to introduce yourself to a stranger, especially not to one as strange as Doctor Black. The man was dressed more like a mortician than a doctor. His filmy eyes sunken deep into his head like that of a mummified corpse.

He glared down at the baby-faced woman. Judging by her cheerful demeanor, the doctor surmised that she too had come from the city. She couldn't have come from the islands. Cheery people did not exist on the islands.

"That is correct," he said in a firm tone, ocean mist stabbing at his throat. "Please, keep your distance—"

His words were cut short when the woman stuck a penny to his forehead. "What are you..." the doctor began.

Then she pressed a quarter and a dime onto him. The woman smiled as the coins remained embedded into his face.

"It's true," she said. "Your skin really is like silly putty."

He removed the coins from his forehead and tossed them over his shoulder, into the icy gray waves. The three indentations lingered in his flesh, shaped like the faces of presidents.

"It's highly contagious," said the doctor. "You shouldn't touch me."

"I didn't touch you with my fingers," she said. "Besides, your disease isn't as contagious as they say. Only your sweat can infect me, and since most of your pores have been smoothed over you hardly sweat at all."

"It's not worth the risk," said the doctor, turning back toward the sea. "There's no cure. You should leave me alone."

The girl only snickered at him.

"I'll be careful," she said. Her tone of voice was as if she were making fun of him for worrying so much.

When he looked back at her, he peered deep inside her eyes and realized she was a much stronger person than most girls her age. There was a circular scar on her left cheek as if somebody had burned her with a car cigarette lighter as a child. White slits stretched across her throat as if somebody had once attempted to murder her in a dark alleyway but narrowly missed the major blood vessels. She had obviously been through a lot in her short life. He doubted there was much that still frightened her.

"Which island are you going to?" she asked him.

"Siren Cove," he said.

"The one with the mermaids?"

"Yes. I have business there."

"I guess we'll be like neighbors," she said. "I'm going to Green Rock, the next island down."

"I'm unaware of an island called Green Rock."

"It's not an inhabited island. Nothing there but turtles. My father and his assistant have been living there for a few months now, studying the mutations."

Doctor Black nodded. He was familiar with the deformities of some aquatic species in the region, especially the turtles which had been growing extra limbs to resemble stubby hard-shelled arachnids.

"I hate leaving the city," she said. "There's not even internet or cell phone reception out in the islands. But my dad wants to keep an eye on me while school's out for winter break. He's always so worried." She looked up at the young doctor. "How long are you staying in Siren Cove? Maybe I can come visit you sometime and we can see the mermaids together."

"The cove is prohibited to tourists," said the doctor.

"Oh yeah, the Endangered Species Protection Act," she said. "It's kind of bullshit."

"They won't even tolerate documentary filmmakers in the area."

"I know. I wish I could at least see the mermaids on the Discovery Channel. I've only seen early photos."

She looked out at the water, scanning the surface for signs of fish women.

"Do you think they go out as far as Green Rock?" she asked.

"Probably not," he said. "They tend to stay close by their food source. They'd have no interest in an uninhabited island."

"Food source?" she asked. "You mean humans, right?"

"Human males," he said.

"The fishermen from the village?"

The doctor nodded. "The teenage sons of fishermen are the most targeted prey. Not only are they easily lured into the water at that age, but their meat is fresh and tender."

"They don't eat women?"

"They don't usually hunt women, but they might try to if there aren't any males around." He pointed out to sea. "And no one is safe in open water. They don't need to lure swimming prey. They just pull them under the waves and drown them."

"Are they really all that dangerous?" She leaned against the edge of the ship, tapping a box of cigarettes in her pocket.

"Indeed," he said. "They're the only marine animals that specifically target humans for food. You'd be safer swimming with sharks."

She smiled excitedly. "I hope I get to see one someday."

He shook his head at the girl. He always wondered why nobody ever took the danger of mermaids seriously until they were pulled into the water with one.

She giggled at him, as if she knew exactly what he was thinking.

"By the way," the girl turned to him and held out her hand, "I didn't catch your name."

He looked down at her hand.

"Black," he said.

"That's it? Just Black?"

"John Black."

"Well, nice to meet you, John Black," she said. "I'm Jackson. Just Jackson."

She grabbed his hand and shook it, knowing full well he didn't want to shake hands. The doctor didn't care that they were both wearing gloves. He was paranoid about spreading his disease. He couldn't bear the idea of transmitting such a grotesque malady to another human being.

All the other passengers were dropped off on the larger, more populated islands in the area. Only Jackson and Doctor Black remained on the ship with the boatman for the long stretch of ocean toward Siren Cove. The sky grew darker the closer they got to the island. The fog became so thick they could hardly see where they were going.

"They really are isolated out here," Jackson said.

"The three hour journey from the mainland keeps the village hidden away from the rest of the world."

"Must be lonely," she said.

Jackson didn't want to think about how her destination was even further out there, even more isolated from the world.

The cold air caused her nose to run. She wiped it with her red gloves as she asked, "Do you think I'll get to see any mermaids when we dock?"

The doctor shrugged. "We'll be going through their waters soon, but it's doubtful. They're very shy creatures. You usually only see them during mating season or if they're hunting you as prey."

"Does it happen to be mating season?"

"Far from it."

"They mate with humans, right? That's why you see them more during mating season, because they're looking for human males to mate with?"

He shook his head. "That's a myth, actually. They don't mate with humans."

"But there are no mermen," she said. "How do they reproduce?"

"There are male mermaids, but most people can't tell them apart from the females. You have to remember that mermaids are not half human. They are one hundred percent fish. They've evolved to resemble human females in order to lure their prey to them. Below the waist, they have either male or female fish anatomy. They reproduce oviparously. Mating with a mermaid would be no different than attempting to mate with a tuna."

"So they're not human at all?"

"No, even their upper halves are more fish than human when you study them up close. They have the eyes of fish, their skin is firm and rubbery like that of a shark, they have gills hiding beneath their hair, cold blood running in their veins."

"And they are still able to seduce men to their deaths?"

"Precisely. Within close proximity, a mermaid will release powerful pheromones into the air that cause a reaction in human males. It's like a powerful aphrodisiac. Although most women can resist them, these chemicals will put a male into a heightened sexual state. He won't be able to resist her, even if he's completely aware that he's about to be killed."

Jackson chuckled out loud. She probably knew quite a few guys in college who would be easy prey for mermaids. Before she could ask the doctor another question about the fish women, a thunderous crashing sound echoed through the frame of the ship. The vessel came to a halt and tipped slightly to the side.

"What happened?" Jackson cried. Her cheerfully confident attitude became replaced with alarm. "Did we hit something?"

A squealing noise vibrated through the ship.

17

"I think we've run aground." He hurried toward the front of the ship, gesturing to the girl to follow him. "Quickly."

Their driver was in a panic, hitting the gas, messing with the controls. He was an older Brazilian man with a thick gray beard and lips that crumbled with dead skin.

"What's wrong?" the doctor asked him. He had to speak up. The engine was roaring.

"I don't know," said the boatman in a thick accent, trying to steer the ship away from whatever was pinning them down. "Big problem."

"What did we hit?"

"Nothing."

"Certainly you had to have hit something."

"We couldn't have. There's nothing here. Unless we hit whale."

"You should realize the considerable amount of danger we'll be in if this boat sinks," said the doctor. "These are mermaid infested waters."

The boatman hit the gas again and the ship chugged forward.

"That's it," said the boatman. He looked back at the doctor with a nervous smile. "It's good. We'll get there. No worry."

The boat continued on toward land, moving at a third of the pace.

The doctor let out a sigh. He looked overboard, scanning the water for mermaids, just in case. There were none to be seen. But the fog was thick. Just because he didn't see any didn't mean they weren't there.

"Do you think the mermaids caused it?" Jackson asked him.

"They're too small to be of any harm to a ship this size," he said.

"But what if they set a trap?" she asked. "Maybe they pulled some kind of debris in the way of the ship."

The doctor shook his head. "Remember, they're only fish. They have the brains of fish. They don't have the intelligence to plan anything like that."

The boat moved slower and slower as it went. A loud rumbling noise rippled from the engine. The vessel seemed like it was going to fall apart at any moment.

"Are we going to make it?" Jackson asked.

"I don't know," said the doctor. "The island is still half an hour away and we're taking on water fast."

When they made it to the dock, the boat was flooded and barely staying afloat. The two passengers removed their luggage as the boatman stood on the pier, examining the massive hole in his ship.

"What could have caused this?" the boatman asked Doctor Black, pointing at the damage beneath the water. "Big swordfish?"

The hole was almost perfectly circular and traveled all the way through the ship from one side to the other. It seemed as if somebody shoved a spear the size of a telephone pole right through it.

"I've never seen anything like it," said the doctor. He seemed more interested than concerned.

"Something really no like boat, eh?" said the boatman, chuckling. "I'll never fix that."

The boat's descent quickened its pace until only the deck could be seen beneath the surface of the water. The boatman laughed drunkenly as it sank, as if he were happy to see it go.

"We're stuck here," said the doctor.

Jackson went to the old man, three backpacks thrown over her shoulder and a large suitcase by her feet. She was annoyed by how lightly he was taking the situation.

"Don't you even care that you just wrecked your boat?" she asked.

The old man shrugged at her. "This is not my boat. It belongs to my brother-in-law. He's an asshole. Fuck his boat."

"How am I getting to Green Rock?" she asked him.

The boatman laughed at her.

"Oh yes," he said. "You're the scientist daughter. It's good. My brother-in-law come get us. You'll be fine."

"How long will that take?" she asked.

"As soon as he gets back from New York, he'll come get us. He'll be so pissed. Fuck him."

"What do you mean when he gets back from New York? How long will that be?"

"Two weeks. No worry."

"Two weeks!"

"It's good. The grays will give us free shelter until then. They're nice people."

"What the hell are the grays?" she asked.

The doctor said, "That's what they call the villagers on this island."

"I'm not staying here for two weeks," she yelled. "My father will freak out if he doesn't hear from me. He'll think I'm dead in a ditch somewhere."

She looked at the old boatman's ass as if she contemplated kicking him in the water.

"Maybe one of the locals will be willing to take you there," said the doctor, the coin-shaped indentations still in his face.

Jackson scanned the area. The place was deserted. The beach was rocky, surrounded by steep hills. There were a couple storage shacks at the end of the pier, but otherwise there was no sign of civilization.

"Where is everyone?" Jackson asked.

The doctor picked up his single suitcase and walked down the pier away from the sunken vessel.

"The village is on the other side of the island," he said. "Outsiders are prohibited from docking at their private harbor in the cove, due to the mermaids." He pointed back at the sunken ship. "This area is where they normally receive supplies from the mainland."

The boatman followed after them and chuckled.

"Their supplies are underwater now," he said. "No shipment for grays this month."

Then he took a swig of gin from a pint-sized bottle hiding in his pocket.

They took the trail leading into the hills. The fog came in so thick they couldn't make out much of the island around them as they traveled. They could hardly even make out that it was still daytime.

"So why are the villagers called grays?" Jackson asked the doctor.

"Because of their skin," he said.

"They have gray-colored skin?" she asked.

"They have no color in their skin at all," he said. "Nor in their hair or eyes. They are completely monochrome. It's a hereditary trait unique to this village."

"They're black and white people?" she asked.

"Even their blood and internal organs lack color," said the doctor. "It's as if somebody pulled them out of an old black and white movie into our world."

"How is that possible?"

"They say it's the island that does it to people," said the doctor. "It's such a cold, lonely place that it sucks all color out of your heart and soul. Then it sucks all color from your flesh and blood."

"A local myth?" she asked.

"Exactly," said the doctor. "It's most likely just an illusion caused by the lack of sunlight in this region. The right lighting can make anyone appear gray."

The sound of engines roared in the distance when they reached the top of the hill. Out of the fog, three people on ATVs rode out toward them. They wore bright blue and red outfits. The one in the front had rainbow-colored feathers poking out of the top of his helmet like a flamboyant Trojan warrior.

As she saw them coming closer, Jackson turned to the doctor and said, "I thought you said they have no color?"

The doctor rubbed the wrinkles out of his top coat and straightened his long-brimmed hat.

"The younger generations on the island try to offset the lack of color in their skin by wearing bright clothing," said the doctor. "But it doesn't seem to help much."

When the motorcycles pulled over in front of them, Jackson realized the clothing wasn't as bright as she first thought. Even the rainbow feathers looked dull and faded as the lead driver removed the helmet from his head.

"Doctor Black?" He was a large man of about thirty, small eyes, pointy nose and sharp cheek bones. As he came toward them, he held out his hand, "I saw the ship coming in."

"Stephen," said the doctor. He raised his hands to show he was uncomfortable touching him. "It's been a long time."

"Too long," said the gray man.

"We had a bit of trouble on the way," said the doctor. "Something hit the boat and put a rather large hole through the bow. We barely made it here."

"Where is it now?" Stephen asked, looking at the boatman. "Can I be of any assistance?"

"It's done for," said the boatman, shaking his head. "It sunk to the bottom of the lagoon."

"And our supplies?" asked the young man.

The boatman pointed his thumb downward and coldly responded, "Nope."

A look of worry spread across the young man's face, but he

tried his best not to show it.

"That's a terrible pity," he said. "We're in desperate need of food."

"Because of your problem?" asked the doctor.

He nodded. "No one in the village is willing to go anywhere near the water anymore, even to fish. Not since the merchows stopped doing their job."

"That's precisely why I'm here," Black said.

"And we're very grateful you came on such short notice," Stephen said. "Especially with your condition."

"I'm just doing my job," said the doctor. "Plus, I promised your father I'd come straight away if you ever had any issues with the merchows my company provided for you."

The gray man nodded. "Well, thanks for coming. You're desperately needed."

"How is your father, anyway?" asked the doctor.

Stephen looked away, toward his sisters on the bikes behind him. They lowered their heads. When he looked back, the doctor saw it on his face.

"He passed away last month," said Stephen. "I've replaced him as village chief."

Doctor Black didn't want to question it, but he was sure he knew the cause of the old chief's death. It wasn't natural causes, that's for sure. The old man was stronger and healthier than anyone a third his age.

The doctor pointed to the young woman beside him. "This is Jackson. She's trying to get to Green Rock. Do you know of anyone who could take her out there?"

The young village chief looked at the girl. "You must be Trent Jackson's daughter." As she nodded, he shook his head. "I'm sorry, but I can't be of much assistance to you. Nobody has been willing to go out to sea in weeks. Not since the chief died. You can try asking around, but I doubt you'd find anyone to agree. Not unless the doctor here can solve our problem."

Jackson looked at the doctor.

23

"I'll see what I can do," said Black. "But my investigation could take time."

"Let me know if you need any help," said the chief. "The entire village is at your disposal. We'll do everything it takes to get this fixed and send you back home to your family."

"That won't be necessary," said the doctor and the chief looked at him with a confused face. "It will be good to reunite this girl with her father, but I don't plan to go back home."

"What do you mean?" asked the chief. "The next supply ship is due to pick you up in three weeks."

"You might want to cancel my ticket if you've already paid for it," said the doctor. "I'm in the late stages of Zimmer's Disease. I only have a week to live, at most."

The chief didn't know how to respond to that, breaking eye contact with the tall man in black. He looked back at his sisters and then smiled nervously.

"Surely, they could have sent somebody else," said the chief. "You have a wife and daughter, don't you? Shouldn't you be with them for your final days?"

The doctor shook his head. "There wasn't anyone else they could send but me. If I refused, the company would have fired me and my daughter would not receive benefits after my death. It was an easy decision."

"I'm sorry..." said the chief.

"Don't be," said Doctor Black. "My family said their goodbyes yesterday evening, after cheesecake. I've made peace with the universe. Now I have a job to do."

The chief nodded awkwardly. He stuttered and pointed at the backseats on the ATVs, "Come with us. We'll take you into town."

"Good," the doctor said, sitting on the back of the motorcycle driven by the chief's younger sister. "I'd like to get to work as soon as possible."

The chief bowed to Jackson and the boatman, and pointed them toward the ATVs. The doctor and the chief's sister didn't wait for the others, roaring down the hill, mud spraying in their wake.

The village was a bit more modern than the visitors were expecting. More than eighty houses lined the hillside, all of them painted bright purple, pink, and blue. They had electricity and satellite television, heated pools and mowed lawns.

When they got to the center of town, they stepped off of their bikes and had a look around.

"It's much different than last time I was here," said the doctor.

The chief nodded. "With the money the government's given us we've been able to upgrade our community quite a bit. It was Cheryl's idea to paint all the houses bright colors." He pointed at his older sister with long black hair and a flowery jacket. "It was supposed to cheer the place up. But I don't know… I think it made the place even more depressing."

He didn't seem to care that his sister heard that comment. Cheryl glared at him, ready to attack him even though he was at least twice her size. Black remembered Cheryl was the more moody of the old chief's daughters.

"The three of you can stay next door to my sisters," Stephen said, "in my father's old house. Nobody's been in there since he died, so it might not be in the best condition."

"It'll be fine," Black said. "I take it you've got your own place now?"

The chief nodded. "I moved in with my wife last year." He pointed to a large mansion towering above the rest of the village. "On the cliff overlooking the sea."

"So you're married now?" asked the doctor. "To the same girl you were with when I came last?"

He shook his head. "Not her. Laura moved away years ago, like most young people do when they come of age. No, this is somebody you've never met before. She's not from here."

The chief's 25-year-old sister, Amy, with light gray hair and pouty black lips took the doctor by the arm.

She said, "He met her on the mainland while in college."

The doctor tried to pull himself away from the woman, but she held him tight. He could feel her arm creating an indentation in his flesh through his coat sleeve.

"I didn't know anyone from Siren Cove needed to attend college," the doctor said.

"Well, I did." He smiled proudly. "I even got a master's degree. My father thought the next chief should have a higher education, for the sake of the village."

The doctor agreed.

"Enough with small talk," the boatman said, pointing his empty gin bottle at the ground. "Do you have any booze in this place?"

The chief patted the old man on the shoulder.

"We're dangerously short on all other supplies," said the chief. "But booze is one thing we always have in abundance."

"God bless you, sir," said the boatman. "You'll hear no complaints from me during my stay as long as you keep the liquor flowing."

The chief unlocked his father's home, a bright purple building surrounded by dead rose bushes. He wouldn't enter with them, nor would his sisters. They waited outside until their visitors found their rooms and dropped off their bags.

"Ready to go?" the chief asked the doctor from the doorway.

The doctor tipped the brim of his hat in response.

The chief looked at the other two guests. "You two can stay here. We have business to attend to with the doctor."

Jackson glanced back at the boatman. He had already broken

into a bottle of wine he found in the kitchen.

"I think I'd rather go with you if that's okay," Jackson said.

"It's okay with me as long as the doctor doesn't mind," said the chief.

Black paused for a moment to think it over. Then he looked at her. "Since you'll be on the island for a while, you're going to see them sooner or later. You'll have to sign a confidentiality agreement."

"Sure," Jackson said. "Whatever you want."

The doctor nodded.

"Let's go," he told the chief. "We don't have much daylight left."

He took a deep breath of sea air as he looked out to the harbor at the end of the street.

"Not much daylight left at all."

The younger sister stayed behind. She appeared too frightened to accompany them. Jackson was curious about what unnerved her as she followed Cheryl, Stephen, and Doctor Black toward the harbor.

The area at the end of the street was fenced off and locked. This was to prevent village children from journeying too close to the water.

"What you're about to see is not to be made public," the doctor told the young woman, as the chief opened the gate and let them through.

"I understand," Jackson said.

"It's not something that most people in our society would find acceptable," said the doctor. "But it's absolutely necessary. There's no other way around it."

"What are you talking about?" Jackson asked.

"Merchow," said the chief, pointing at a group of villagers

that were gathered by the shore.

"Merchow?"

"That's the local term for them," the doctor said. "They are also referred to as *food people* in my industry."

Jackson looked carefully at the group of people in front of them. They were not members of the village. They appeared to be more like prisoners, wandering along the shore with their wrists bound. They were mostly naked, wearing simple loincloths. Their skin was a dark reddish brown, as if from being out in the sun all the time.

"Food people?" Jackson asked.

"Human livestock," said the chief. "They're used as food for the mermaids."

"You feed people to mermaids?" Jackson cried. "Real human beings?"

The doctor could tell the idea was already upsetting the girl. It was a reaction he was very used to seeing in his line of work. The doctor proceeded to explain, in a calm, impassive manner.

"Humans are the mermaids' only food source," said the doctor. "If they don't eat they will die. It's the only way to protect their species from extinction."

"Don't you think that's taking environmentalism a little too far?" Jackson asked.

The doctor shook his head. "Not at all. Many of the food people are volunteers. They've given their lives in order to protect the mermaid species."

"What?" she found the idea absurd. "Well, what about the others?"

"Most of the others were murderers, rapists, and terrorists," said the doctor. "They've lost their rights to be human. Becoming food people is how they repay their debt to society."

"This is insane," Jackson said. "They're only fish. You don't feed people to fish, even criminals."

Jackson wanted to turn around and walk away, but she couldn't take her eyes off the merchow. They looked like they were no longer human. Their heads shaved bald. Their eyes were those of animals. They ate from troughs like man-shaped pigs, snorting and squealing but no longer capable of language.

CHAPTER TWO
THE FOOD PEOPLE

"So the mermaids are no longer eating them?" the doctor asked the chief as they walked up the beach toward the herd of food people.

"No," Stephen said. "They only go after my fishermen. They've taken nearly half of the village men in just the past few months, but not a single merchow. It's almost as if they don't find them appetizing anymore."

The two women followed close behind, not saying a word, keeping their eyes on the shore.

"They won't eat sick men," said the doctor. "That's usually the cause in situations like this. A disease must have spread through the herd."

"Can they be cured?"

"If a disease is what's causing the problem, I'll see what I can do. If they have an incurable disease, the whole herd will likely have to be destroyed and replaced."

"I'm guessing that will be expensive, won't it?"

"The government will likely pay for most of the cost of replacements," he said. "That is, as long as you haven't killed any of the mermaids. For that you'd not only lose all financial support from the government, you'd also be fined, imprisoned, or worse."

"My people haven't killed any of them," said the chief.

"Be sure they don't," said the doctor. "The government does not take these matters lightly. There was one village that slaughtered fourteen mermaids to avenge the death of one missing child. By the end of the month, every member of that community had been transformed into human livestock in order to ensure the survival of the remaining mermaid colony. Remember that."

"I understand," said the chief.

"Were your men taking their pills when they were attacked?"

"Yeah, every time," said the chief. "But the mermaids still took them."

"If they absolutely must go near the water have them double their doses from now on," said the doctor. "Triple if they are heavyset."

"I already told them to," said the chief. "But most of them refuse to do it. They think the pills are turning them into women."

"That is the point. With so much estrogen in their system, the mermaid pheromones will have no effect."

"But it's ruining their sex lives," said the chief.

"Better to lose their lives than their sex lives?"

Stephen shrugged.

"Just keep them away from the water altogether then," said the doctor. "At least until I figure out the cause of this problem."

The doctor and chief chose one male food person to examine. The merchow just stood there drooling at them as the doctor gave him a physical.

"Have they been lobotomized or something?" Jackson asked the doctor, pointing at the distant look in his eyes. "He looks brain dead."

"Not exactly," said the doctor. "They've been genetically transformed. Their intelligence is now equal to that of cattle. Their flesh has been altered in consistency and artificially-flavored to be even more appetizing to mermaids than usual human meat. They're hardly human anymore."

Jackson saw that they weren't all men. Some of the food people were women and children. Many of the females were

31

either pregnant or carrying infants in their arms.

When the chief saw her looking at the young food people with a disgusted look on her face, he said, "The merchows can also reproduce at a faster rate than humans. They're always breeding new generations of livestock to produce more food for the mermaids."

"Someday we won't need to transform humans into food people at all," said the doctor. "They will eventually be able to perpetuate themselves. After a few generations, they'll become a new species of human."

"It's atrocious if you ask me," Jackson said.

Cheryl glared at her as if she wanted to punch her in the stomach. "Nobody asked you."

When Jackson saw the look in the woman's eyes, she decided to let it go. Cheryl had a completely different opinion of the food people. To her, they were salvation. They protected her friends and family from the voracious fish women. They were a blessing.

"So does anything seem wrong with them?" asked the chief.

"Nothing apparent," said the doctor. He sniffed at the merchow's crotch. "They smell healthy enough."

The doctor grabbed a handful of flesh from the merchow's thigh and ripped away a chunk of meat. The flesh was firm yet tender, slipping right off the bone. It was more like smoked salmon than human muscle.

"The consistency is right," he said, squeezing the filet of meat in his hand.

He took a bite and chewed slowly, exploring the flavor with every part of his tongue.

"The taste is right," he said. "The teriyaki flavoring is not overpowering. It's got the perfect balance between fishy and porky."

The doctor spit out the bite and dropped the meat on the ground, wiping his hands together to remove the crumbly flesh. Jackson wondered why the food person's gaping wound didn't bleed or why the creature didn't cry out in pain. She assumed their nervous and circulatory systems must not have been the same as a human's.

"I'll have to run some tests, but these food people appear to be perfectly healthy to me," said the doctor. "Perhaps it's the mermaids who are sick."

The doctor looked at the shoreline. Some of the food people were even wading in the water, but no mermaids came to get them. Anything in the shape of a human should at least draw their attention. It was very unusual behavior for mermaids.

Back at Cheryl and Amy's house, the chief prepared dinner for their guests.

"We don't have much to offer you," said the chief, stirring a pot of stewed potatoes in peppery tomato sauce, "but it's food."

Jackson and the boatman sat at the table with the two village sisters. With their coats and hats off, Jackson could tell just how strange they looked with no color in their skin. They really did have grayish-white flesh. No pinks, no tans, no browns in their pigment. Even the veins crawling up their arms were a dark gray color. They were truly monochrome.

"We've been flying through the preserves from our storage," Amy said. "Our gardens usually provide us with enough food to last through the winter months, but we'll be lucky if we still have a single jar of jelly by the end of next week." She licked her thumb. "It's kind of scary."

The chief carried the pot of stew to the table as Cheryl set bowls and spoons out for the guests.

"Nonsense," said the chief, serving Jackson first with a wooden ladle. "Our Doctor Black will solve the problem in one week's time. Then our freezers will be loaded with halibut and snapper."

"Speaking of Doctor Black, where did he go to?" Amy asked.

"He'll be here shortly," said the chief. "He's just running a few tests."

Just as the chief finished speaking, the doctor stepped through the front door and entered into the circular dining room. He was rubbing his forehead, as if trying to smooth out the coin-shaped indentations that still lingered on his face.

"That didn't take long," said the chief.

"No, it didn't," said the doctor, sitting next to Jackson and pouring himself a bowl of the potato stew. "There are only three diseases that could have possibly been the cause. All of them are unique to the food people species and all three are fairly easy to identify. But after studying the samples I took from your livestock, not a single one of them display symptoms of any of these diseases. It's got to be something else."

Stephen sat down and poured his stew slowly, staring into the red liquid as if contemplating the situation. The young chief had hoped the solution would have been much more easily resolved once the doctor arrived in the village. He didn't like seeing him baffled, even if the doctor had only just begun his investigation.

"I'll not rest until I find a solution," the doctor told Stephen in a confident tone, trying to reassure the obviously frustrated young chief.

Stephen looked up at the doctor and smiled delicately.

"Quite right," Stephen said. "I have the utmost faith in your abilities, Doctor. I'm sure you'll figure out what's wrong soon enough."

Jackson sat quietly next to the boatman. She still could not believe what she had seen back on the beach. Turning humans into food for unintelligent creatures seemed too barbaric to her. Even if they were criminals or volunteers, it was no excuse. The worst part of it all was how commonplace it seemed to the people in her company.

The awkward silence was broken by the sound of a baby screaming in the next room.

"There she goes again," Cheryl whined.

Amy leapt from her chair so fast she nearly knocked the table over.

"I'll get it," she said. Then she looked at the doctor. "Excuse me."

As the younger sibling went in the backroom, the doctor smiled at the chief.

"Amy has a child now?" he asked.

The chief nodded slowly, but didn't look the doctor in the eyes.

"Who's the father?" the doctor asked.

Cheryl glared at him as he asked the question. He quickly realized he had stumbled upon a sore topic.

"The father's dead," Cheryl said. "That's all you need to know."

Jackson stood from the table.

"Where do you think you're going?" Cheryl snapped at the girl.

She pointed at the hallway. "I was just going to see if she needed any help."

"Did anyone ask for your help?"

"No, but…"

"Sit down," Cheryl said. "Let Amy deal with it."

Jackson lowered herself slowly back into her seat. Cheryl took her bowl and left the room, storming out onto the porch.

"I'm sorry," Jackson said, too softly for Cheryl to hear.

The chief turned to the girl. "Don't be. You'll have to forgive my sister. We've lost many of our friends and family as of late. We're all angry and upset over this ugly affair."

"You don't have to explain," Jackson said. "I understand."

The chief continued, "Even once the problem has been solved, our village will never go back to what it once was. Too much has changed."

"I'm sorry," Jackson said. She didn't know what else to say. The chief tried to change the subject.

"So your father's staying on Green Rock?" he asked her.

"Yes," she said. "He's going to be worried sick."

"In the morning, come to my house on top of the hill," he said. "You can contact your father via satellite phone."

"Really?" she asked. "You have a satellite phone?"

"It's the only one in the village," Stephen said. "We won't be able to get you to your father, but at least he'll know you're alright."

"Thank you," she said, smiling with relief. "You have no idea how much that means to me."

"Not a problem," said the chief.

The boatman belched as he licked his bowl clean.

Stephen looked at the boatman as if he'd forgotten all about him. "You can come, too, Mr... what is your name again?"

"I am Oswaldo," said the boatman. He was visibly intoxicated.

"Oswaldo," said the chief. "If you need to contact anyone you can come use the phone in the morning as well."

Oswaldo chuckled at him and said something in Portuguese that the chief could not comprehend.

Without finishing even a third of his food, the chief stood from his seat.

"I should go check on my wife," he said. "She didn't know I would be gone for so long. We'll speak again in the morning, after you've all had a chance to rest."

"I'll see you then," said Doctor Black.

Jackson just smiled awkwardly at the chief as he walked out the door. Without even a goodbye, the chief was gone and the three visitors found themselves alone in the dining room of the strange household.

"So now what?" Jackson said to the doctor.

"I'd like you to help Mr. Oswaldo next door and then get some sleep," said the doctor.

"What about you?" she asked.

The doctor wiped his mouth with a cloth napkin and stood from his seat.

"I still have work to do," he said.

As the doctor walked out the front door, Jackson followed after him.

"Wait," Jackson yelled, running out of the front door after the doctor. "Can I help?"

He turned to her.

She said, "I can never sleep in a strange place and would rather keep busy."

He shook his head. "Absolutely not. It'll be far too dangerous."

"Dangerous? How?"

"There doesn't appear to be anything wrong with the food people, so it must be something wrong with the mermaids. I need to see them."

"At night?" she asked. "All alone?"

"It will be the best time to encounter one," said the doctor. "They are most active at night and tend to only hunt lone men."

"But what if you get killed?" she asked.

"I am a dead man anyway," said the doctor. "I have to risk it. I don't have time to waste."

"Committing suicide won't help anyone," she said.

"Don't worry about it," he said, turning away to walk down the road toward the harbor. "I've taken a triple dose of the hormone drug. They won't be able to seduce me so easily."

"They better not," she yelled.

The doctor just waved at her without turning back.

As Doctor Black climbed the fence and dropped down onto the beach below, he heard the snorting and squealing sounds of the food people. He pulled a flashlight from his coat and shined it on them. Most of them were huddled together for warmth. Two of them were mating in the sand under the pier. Others were spread out, stepping through the ocean water as if begging to be captured by mermaids.

The doctor walked along the beach, shining his light out onto the waves, searching for signs of fish women.

"Nine o'clock p.m., no signs of the mermaids along the coast of Siren Cove," the doctor said into a digital recording device. "Last time I was here, the waters were teeming with them at this hour. I wonder if something has been scaring them away from this particular beach. Perhaps sharks or even jellyfish. I'll keep waiting and see if they show."

The doctor moved closer to the water and kept his eyes open.

After a couple hours of waiting, making himself an easy target for the predators, he said into his recorder, "It doesn't look like they use this beach as a hunting ground anymore. I'm going to wait for them in the harbor close by the fishing boats where the locals have been disappearing." He turned and walked toward the docks. "If this is just a matter of food placement it will be an easy problem to fix."

After only three feet, the doctor saw a human face peek out of the water in the distance. As he shined his light across the surface of the water, its eyes glimmered like those of a cat. Its face was pale green in color. Although he couldn't see much of it, he knew exactly what it was.

He spoke into his recorder, "Disregard that last statement. My first subject has made an appearance."

Then he waited to see if the mermaid would come after him.

CHAPTER THREE
MERMAID KISSES

The mermaid was definitely hunting Doctor Black. She swam through the waves toward him, keeping an eye on his every move.

"It is definitely not the beach that is keeping them away," the doctor said into his recorder. "She shows no signs of hesitation as she approaches."

He watched her for a moment. Her long wet black hair covered her shoulders and fish-like features—the gills on her neck and small holes for ears.

"There are food people all around, but it appears she only has her sights on me. I'm going to move out of the way to verify."

The doctor went down the beach, walking toward the pier. The mermaid swam slowly along the shore beside him. She ignored all of the food people, passing them as if they were invisible.

"She definitely has no interest in any of the food people," he said into the recorder. "She just passed right by one that was standing in the water, a far easier prey. Not only that, but the merchow seem to have no interest in the mermaid. If she is releasing her pheromones it has no effect on the livestock."

The mermaid followed the doctor all the way to the dock. He climbed the steps and walked out on the pier, watching her as she stalked him.

"Judging by the sweet honey-apricot odor in the air, I deduce that she is releasing her pheromones. The smell is much sweeter than my previous encounters with mermaids in this region."

The mermaid dove beneath the water and slapped her fishtail, splashing the doctor in a flirtatious manner. The doctor always found it curious how mermaids attempted to lure their prey by splashing them with their fishtails.

"Now she's spraying me with pheromone-infused ocean water to further the seduction," said the doctor. "I can already feel the effect as it is absorbed by my skin. The hormone pills are keeping my mind sober. If I had not taken precautionary measures, it would have already been too late for me to turn back."

The mermaid rolled in the water to give the doctor a quick glimpse of her human-shaped breasts. The nipples were a dark shade of green.

"A curious thing," the doctor said into the recorder. "I just saw human-shaped nipples protruding from the subject's mammary glands. This is uncharacteristic of the mermaids from this region, who all had smooth nipple-less breasts."

The doctor walked to the edge of the pier. The mermaid dove beneath the water and didn't resurface.

"I've lost the subject's position, but based on the smell intensifying around me I assume she must be close by."

Doctor Black shined his light on the water but didn't see any sign of the fish woman. He sat down on the edge of the dock. Then he placed his recorder next to him in a dry, safe spot. Just in case the mermaid caught him off guard and knocked him over the side of the pier, there would still be documentation of what had happened to him.

"Where did you go off to?" the doctor spoke to the water, waiting patiently by the edge of the pier. "Don't run away, you haven't had your dinner yet."

She poked her head up in the water a dozen yards away.

"What are you doing way out there?" he asked the mermaid, waving her over. "Come closer."

The mermaid swam back and forth, exposing her breasts, splashing her tail.

"I'm not going to swim out to you," the doctor told her. "You have to come to me."

The mermaid dove under the water again.

The doctor said into the recorder, "The subject is attempting to lure me into the water through visual stimulation. It is having no effect on me whatsoever."

The mermaid's face emerged closer to the doctor, staring at him with cold black eyes.

"Hello beautiful," the doctor said to the mermaid. "Are you hungry?"

The mermaid swam slowly to the doctor, almost cautiously. Her glossy eyes shimmered at him.

"That's my girl," he said to the fish. "Come and eat."

She came right up to him, staring him in the eyes.

"The subject is surprisingly gentle," the doctor said to his recorder. "Not ferocious or aggressive. This is most likely a sign that she's well-fed."

The mermaid came up to the pier and raised her hands to him. Long black talons curled from her fingertips.

"Now she's right in front of me, inviting me into her arms," said the doctor. "My first impression of the subject is that she's a very healthy specimen. No visible sign of disease or malnutrition."

He examined the mermaid more carefully. His light reflected against her shiny black hair and glistening pale-green flesh.

"You sure are a beautiful creature, aren't you?" he said to the fish.

The mermaid grabbed onto the edge of the pier and lifted herself slightly out of the water toward the doctor.

"Hold on a minute," he said into the recorder.

Something was leaking from her eyes.

"She appears to be crying a black fluid similar to squid ink."

The doctor removed his glove and reached out. The mermaid

closed her eyes as he wiped the black liquid from one of her cheeks.

"The fluid's texture is unique," said the doctor, rubbing it between his fingers. "It feels closer to mucus than ink. It could be a symptom of a new disease. I'm taking a sample. "

The doctor used a cotton swab to capture more of the black fluid. The mermaid just leaned in to him, allowing him to touch her face. She did not react aggressively, but she did move her mouth toward his hand as he took the sample. She kissed his thumb with her rubbery green lips.

"Hold on a minute," he said to the recorder, as he sealed the swab into a plastic tube. "There's something unusual about her teeth."

He placed his fingers beneath her lips and spread them apart, revealing an elongated fang.

"What beautiful sharp teeth," the doctor said, rubbing the fang with the side of his thumb. They were like those of a snake or vampire bat.

"I suspect that the subject is not the same species of mermaid usually found in these waters. Her front fangs closely resemble those of the nagas of southern Europe. I believe this is a completely new species of mermaid."

Four spiky appendages extended from the fish woman's shoulders. When the doctor saw them his eyes widened.

"Yes, I'm positive this is a new species we're dealing with." He rubbed the palm of his hand against one of the appendages and it curled in his fingers. "On the subject's upper arms, there are four small limbs that closely resemble the legs of a crustacean, such as a lobster or crab. I suspect their purpose is to secure their prey during capture."

The mermaid took his hand away from her crab-like appendage and gripped it tightly.

"No," the doctor told her, as she pulled on his arm. "Let go. Bad mermaid."

She dropped into the water and he lunged forward, holding

onto the edge of the pier with his other hand.

"The subject has got a hold of my hand and is trying to pull me into the water with her," he said. "Her manner is still gentle, not aggressive."

Her eyes stared hungrily at him, sucking him toward her, as she continued pulling on him. The doctor became dizzy and drugged.

"I've just realized that I've made a huge error of judgment," the doctor said to the recorder, trying to regain his bearings. "The pheromones of this species have a much stronger effect than any other species on record. The hormone pills I've taken are not powerful enough, even in triple dosage. I also believe the black fluid dripping from the subject's eyes is not a symptom of a disease, but a concentrated aphrodisiac."

He took a deep breath and then said, "As much as I try, I'm no longer able to resist the subject."

The doctor removed his pants and coat as best he could with one arm. Then he offered his other hand to the mermaid.

"As I feed myself to the subject, I'm going to continue recording up until the last minute, so that my successor has complete documentation of what transpired here."

The fish woman took the doctor's other hand and pulled him closer. He slid off of the pier into the water. It was freezing, but his mind was so drugged he could hardly feel anything.

"I'm still amazed by how gentle the subject treats her food," the doctor said. "She has me in the water but has yet to attack."

The mermaid led him away from the pier, swimming backward, her tail slowly flapping below them.

Then she wrapped her arms around him, squeezing her breasts tightly against his chest.

He spoke loud enough for the recorder to pick up his voice,

"Now in her embrace, I understand the purpose of the nipples on this species of mermaid. They are very similar to the suction cups of an octopus or squid. Just by embracing her, my upper torso is literally glued to her body. It would require a tremendous amount of strength to separate us."

She continued staring into his eyes. Ink dripped from her cheeks onto his lips and chest. Then the crab-like appendages closed around his neck and shoulders, fastening him to the mermaid like seatbelts.

"Now the crustacean limbs have captured me, pressing me tightly toward her jaws. Their purpose is definitely to secure the prey. No matter how much I struggle, there would be no possible way to free myself even while being eaten alive. This is much more efficient than the previous mermaid species."

The mermaid rubbed his lower back and kissed his neck and cheeks. The doctor kissed her back, sucking her rubbery lips into his mouth.

"She is now tasting my sweat and saliva, probably to make sure I'm not poisoned or rotten. Her kisses are not offensively fishy, but definitely do not resemble the flavor of a human woman."

The doctor allowed his drugged mind to take over, kissing the fish's gilled neck and sucking on its overly long gooey tongue.

"I believe she's now going to take me under," he said. "Whoever gets this message, please use it only for scientific purposes. My only request is that it does not get into the hands of my daughter. I'd prefer she believe I died peacefully."

As the doctor relaxed into the mermaid's arms, he was taken beneath the waves. The fish whipped her tail, diving deep into the sea. Then she sunk her fangs deep into the doctor's neck and gorged herself on his blood. He closed his eyes and accepted his fate.

But the second she tasted his blood, the mermaid jerked her face away from him. She released him from her crab-grippers and kicked him off of her suction cups with a slap of her tail.

The doctor found himself floating alone in the water, gripping the bite wound on his neck. He swam up to the surface and back to the beach. Soaking wet and freezing in the winter wind, he gathered up his clothes and equipment on the pier.

"Still alive," he said into the recording device, his teeth chattering. "I guess she didn't like the taste of me."

Then he slid the recorder into his soggy pocket and went back toward the village.

Back at the house, he warmed his naked body with a space heater and then examined himself in the bathroom mirror. The mermaid's hand prints were embedded in his back, her breasts created craters in his ribcage, and her fangs left two large holes in his neck. He sighed at the damage and then began the long process of re-sculpting his clay-like flesh back to its original state.

In the morning, Doctor Black felt incredibly hungover. The chemical effects of the mermaid's tears had given him withdrawal pains as they left his system. It was not something he had heard of before, but no other mermaid species were nearly as intoxicating.

The second he got to his feet he had to run to the bathroom to vomit the previous night's dinner. It was like poison.

"Ha ha ha!" Oswaldo said from the living room, eating a bowl of stale fruit loops. "You too?"

Judging by the stains on the old man's shirt, the doctor deduced that he too had been puking all morning.

"I just need water," the doctor said, turning on the tap in the kitchen.

"No water," Oswaldo said.

The doctor drank fermented orange juice instead.

"Where's Jackson?" the doctor asked, pulling on his freezing wet top coat over a dry suit.

The boatman shrugged.

The doctor left the house and took a deep breath of the crisp air. Filling his lungs with the coldness helped his hangover a little.

A crowd of black and white villagers with motley-colored clothing gathered at the end of the block.

"Good morning," the doctor said as he passed an old couple on his way toward the beach.

They did not respond, freezing in their tracks at the sight of him. Perhaps they weren't expecting to see an outsider on the island.

At the end of the road, the chief argued with a group of villagers. They shouted and pushed at each other, these big burly men with bristly gray beards wearing pink sweaters. When he saw the doctor, Stephen stepped away from his people and held up his hands.

"We didn't do it," the chief yelled. "You have to believe me."

The doctor had no idea what the man was talking about until he saw what the villagers were gathered around. Hanging upside-down from hooks, there were three dead mermaids. All of them looked as if they died violently.

CHAPTER FOUR
DEAD FISH

The mermaids varied in age and size, from a three-foot adolescent to a full-grown adult. Their hair tangled around starfish and broken crab shells. Their human flesh was dried to their bones and already reeked of rotten fish.

The doctor stormed through the crowd of villagers to examine the bodies. "How could you let this happen? Who killed them?"

The chief was in a panic. "Nobody killed them. They washed up on the shore this morning. They were already dead."

"Do you know how serious this is?" the doctor said.

"It must have been sharks," said the chief.

The doctor looked at the wounds on the bodies more carefully. They definitely weren't shark bites. Their throats had been ripped open and they had several stab-like wounds all over their body.

"It wasn't sharks," the doctor said, rubbing his gloved fingers across one of the adolescent's holes. "It's very rare for a shark to attack a mermaid, let alone three at once."

The doctor noticed the mermaids were not like the one he encountered the night before. They didn't have fangs or grasping appendages. They belonged to the original species of mermaid found in the region. He wondered if they were attacked by the new species. It was not uncommon for mermaid species to kill each other off in order to eliminate the competition for food. However, the wounds did not look like they came from mermaid bites. The fang marks would have been apparent. The wounds looked more like they were inflicted by harpoons or bladed weapons.

"There will have to be an investigation," said the doctor. "I'll be reporting the incident later this evening."

"Reporting it?"

"You should know just how bad this will be for you if it turns out your people are responsible. Those who work for Endangered Species Security are not very understanding or forgiving in these situations. They care very little for human life."

"But why do you have to report it?" said the chief, his face flushed. "I promise you, it had nothing to do with us. My people are completely aware of the consequences. They would never do such a thing."

"That's not up to me to decide," said the doctor.

The chief glared at him.

The doctor turned away. He had already made up his mind.

"But you know what they'll do to us if you report this," said the chief. "They'll blame it on us whether we did it or not."

"I'm sorry," said the doctor. "If I don't report it I'll be the one they'll blame. And because I'll be dead by the time of the trial it will be my family that will have to pay the consequences for my crime. I cannot allow this to happen."

"You can't just turn us in," said the chief. "You have to help us. At least explain to them that you don't think we're responsible. Give them a reason to doubt we're the cause."

The doctor looked at the mermaid corpses and then back at the chief.

"Put them on ice," said the doctor. "I'll autopsy them later. If I can prove they weren't hunted by your people then I won't have to report the incident."

The chief bowed at him.

"Thank you, doctor," he said. "I promise you'll find it wasn't us."

"That's yet to be seen," said the doctor. "But at least I'll keep a more open mind than Endangered Species Security."

The chief nodded, smiling with relief. Although he was

thankful, all of the other villagers standing behind him looked like they wanted to rip the doctor's guts out.

Doctor Black was worried about Jackson. She was not at the house that morning, nor with the other villagers on the beach. He wandered through the village looking for her, just to be sure she was okay. There was very little he knew about this new species of mermaid. It was possible they had the ability to lure women just as much as they could men. He hoped she didn't go anywhere near the water alone.

While walking through dirt roadways, passing bright purple and pink homes, the doctor came across a small boy no older than his own daughter. He stood in a yard filled with weeds, staring at the prickly bushes, wearing nothing but muddy jeans and sneakers. His gray skin appeared to have been covered in what looked like soot as he scratched himself with his crusty bloody fingernails.

"Boy, over here," the doctor said.

The boy didn't look at him. He pulled bugs out of the bushes and put them in his mouth.

"I'm looking for a young woman by the name of Jackson. She would be a stranger to the village. Have you seen her?"

When the boy turned to him, chewing up a mouthful of grasshoppers, the doctor saw the child's face was horribly deformed and twisted. His cheek and forehead were mangled as if his flesh had been horribly burned. The side of his head was black and charred. He was missing one eye.

"Your face appears to be hideously damaged," said the doctor. "Come to me. I might be able to help you."

The boy did not come to him. He opened his mouth and ate another squirming grasshopper. The doctor took a step closer, to get a better look at him. In the gaping hole where his left eye should have been, a beehive of scabs and crusted mucus pulsed and popped with movement, infested with dozens of tiny black bugs.

"Tell me what caused this affliction," the doctor said.

The charred section of the boy's face appeared to be spreading, the blackness moving across his face, eating away his skin.

"Momma says you're the devil," the boy said.

The doctor was thrown off by the sound of the child's voice. It was raspy, more like a hiss.

"Who is your mother?" the doctor asked.

"Momma says you're the devil," the boy said.

As the blackness moved across the boy's lips, the doctor reached out to grab the boy by the arm. But the boy jumped backward. He ran into the bushes and disappeared deep into the yard. Doctor Black called out to him, but he didn't hear a sound, not even the rustling of dead weeds.

The doctor walked along the side of the yard toward the front of the house. The place was a faded olive green color. The walls were cracked. Weeds grew through the crumbling concrete porch. It didn't look like anyone had lived there in years. The doctor took one more look to see if he could spot the boy, then he moved on down the street.

The doctor found Jackson soon after the encounter with the wounded boy. She was on the road up ahead, walking toward him. Her eyes on her feet. Her arms wrapped around herself. There was definitely something upsetting her.

"Jackson," the doctor said, as their paths crossed.

She looked up at him.

"Is something the matter?" he asked.

She shook her head. "It's probably nothing."

"What?" he asked.

The doctor changed directions so that he could walk alongside her.

"I've been trying to reach my father all morning, but he's not answering," she said.

The doctor nodded. "He's a busy man, isn't he? Wouldn't it make sense that he wouldn't pick up the phone?"

"You don't know my dad," she said. "He worries. He was expecting me last night. It wouldn't be like him to not pick up the phone."

"Just keep trying to reach him," said the doctor. "It's only morning. There could be any number of reasons why he can't pick up the phone."

"I guess you're right. But it's frustrating. I don't like being stranded here like this. I can't reach anyone, no one knows where I am, and none of the villagers will take me anywhere."

The doctor nodded. He felt bad for the girl.

"Tell you what," he said. "If you don't get a hold of your father by this afternoon I'll convince the chief to lend me a boat. I'll take you to Green Rock myself."

"Really?" she asked, her smile returning.

"It won't be a problem. I'd like to have a talk with him anyway."

Then Jackson's smile fell from her face again. Her mouth dropped open. The doctor didn't understand what her reaction was all about until he saw what she was looking at.

Behind them, through the kitchen window of a bright blue home, a food person was hanging from a hook, carved up like a thanksgiving turkey.

"What the hell?" Jackson cried.

The food person's legs and one arm had been severed. The meat from its chest and thighs had been removed. Its scraps lay in the dog bowl. Through another window, they saw a family of five sitting down for breakfast. The looks on their faces were very casual, as if what they were eating was a normal meal of smoked salmon and eggs, as if it was something they had grown accustomed to serving at family meals.

"They're eating it," Jackson said. "They're eating a food person."

The doctor just nodded, as if it were not disturbing at all. "They've been trapped here for weeks with nothing else to eat. Since the food people aren't doing their job, at least they're being put to some use."

He opened up the compost container at the front of their yard. There were skulls and ribcages piled into the pot among other rotting food scraps. The bones were not as rigid as normal human bones. They were softer and almost translucent, like the bones of fish.

"They've been living off of them for a while now, it seems," said the doctor. "I'm sure it's the same with many households in the village."

"But…" Jackson was flabbergasted. "Isn't that cannibalism? They used to be human beings."

"Not anymore," said the doctor. "They've been completely transformed into an entirely different species. They are more like people-shaped cows. In fact, even cows are more intelligent. The intelligence of merchow is closer to that of birds or fish."

"But they used to be human," she said. "That was once a man who gave up his life to feed mermaids, not humans."

"In other circumstances, I would agree that it is a waste of human life. But the villagers are desperate. It's better than starvation."

"I can't believe you're fine with this. It's sick."

"I work for the company that makes them. The idea of consuming food people flesh is no longer disturbing to me. In fact, in a generation or two, once the food people are completely capable of multiplying through normal breeding processes, my company plans to market them for human consumption."

Jackson's mouth dropped open.

"Are you fucking with me?"

Jackson's voice was so loud that she was heard by the monochrome family inside the blue house. They stared at her through the glass for a moment, and then the father stood from his seat and closed the curtains. He had an annoyed look on his face, as if he thought she was incredibly rude for interrupting their family meal.

The doctor moved away from the house, continuing his stroll down the street with the girl.

"It will be strange at first but everyone will get used to the idea soon enough," said the doctor. "If they are bred like cattle people will start thinking of them as cattle. It's not any more disgusting than eating beef or pork or other living things."

Jackson shook her head and groaned loudly.

"I don't know who's weirder, you or these villagers," she said.

"They're not that strange when you get to understand them," said the doctor.

"Actually, I didn't think they were all that strange when I first met them, but the more I get to know them, the stranger they're getting. The chief's wife for instance..."

"You've met the chief's wife?"

Jackson nodded. "I went to the chief's house to call my father. As soon as I got there, the chief refused to let me in. It seemed like he didn't recognize me or forgot that he offered to let me use his phone. Then he had to rush away due to some village emergency. He told me to use his phone in the side yard and to leave it on the porch when I was finished."

"And that's where you met his wife?"

"Well, I didn't actually talk to her," Jackson said. "I saw her looking at me from the upstairs window. She wouldn't take her eyes off of me. And she had this horrible look on her face, as if she wanted to strangle me to death."

"I heard the chief's wife is incredibly shy," said the doctor. "That's why they built their house away from the rest of the village. Seeing an outsider in her yard might have been upsetting to her."

"It's not just that," Jackson said. "She seemed bruised up and battered. There were stitches in her face. At first, I thought she was being abused by her husband, but the more I looked at her the more the wounds seemed self-inflicted. I think she's severely mentally ill."

The doctor strolled quietly after hearing her words, mulling over what she had just told him.

"It's best not to jump to conclusions," the doctor said.

Then he told her not to pry into the personal affairs of the villagers.

"Isolated communities like Siren Cove have their own way of dealing with their problems," he said. "You might want to just forget about what you've seen."

When the doctor was ready to autopsy the dead mermaids, an old village woman led him to where they were being held.

"The men did not kill the mermaids," said the old woman. She was well over a hundred. A lumpy, twisted woman with hardly any white hair left on her head, her facial skin sagging like it was ready to slip off her face. "I've lived here since before these houses had electricity, before the boats had engines. In all this time, none of them have ever killed a single mermaid."

Her name was Ethel. The doctor met her on his last visit to the island. She was the village elder and everyone referred to her as *Grandma* due to the fact that she was the great grandmother or great great grandmother to nearly half the population of the island. There was a local legend about her that said she would never die.

"There's always a first time for everything," said the doctor.

The doctor held her by the arm as she hobbled through the sand toward the warehouses. She was not too shy to lean most of her weight on him. She was not scared of his disease in the slightest.

"I know my people," the woman said. "They used to worship the sea women like gods. I saw my own brother sacrificed to them when I was a girl. It was our way before you came with your food people. We fear and respect them far too much to kill them, even for revenge."

"Then what do you suppose killed them?" asked the doctor.

"I wouldn't know," she said. "The sea is a mysterious place. I've lived here my whole life, only leaving the island once and that was just to visit a hospital on a neighboring island, and the things that have come out of the sea have never ceased to amaze me. Shelled creatures, spiny creatures, creatures with teeth the size of knives; there's all manner of monsters that come up from the depths. Anything could have killed those sea women."

"But not people?"

"Not *my* people." She said, "Except maybe…"

"Except maybe what?"

"Never mind." The woman shook her head and pointed at the old warehouse in front of his. "We've arrived. Your bodies are in the fish storage, through those doors."

The doctor didn't let the woman leave until she explained herself. He got in front of her, stared her in her hollow gray eyes.

"Except maybe what?"

Ethel shook her head. "One person in this village hasn't been himself lately, ever since he came back from the mainland."

"Who? You mean Stephen?"

"Watch yourself around the young chief," said the woman. "He's not been himself lately."

"So you think he could have killed the mermaids?" The doctor couldn't believe it. "He's the only one on this island I trust."

"Don't trust the young chief," said the old woman. "All the men who trust him always turn up dead."

The old woman turned to walk away.

"What do you mean they always turn up dead?"

But she kept moving, hobbling through the sand back to the village.

The warehouse was a giant refrigerator used for storing fish. A rusted ancient structure the size of a church that was usually stacked to the ceiling with fresh meat. Now it was empty, all but for the bodies of three mermaids lying across the cutting room tables. The room could not get cold enough to suppress their rotting stench.

"Fish, fish, fish, fish, fish, fish, fish."

There was somebody else in the cold storage with Doctor Black. An old fisherman with a grimy white beard stepped out of the shadows and approached the mermaids. He had a crooked glass eye that did not look even slightly natural, more like the eye of a child's doll, the bright cartoonish blue eye color clashing with his monochrome features, its size slightly too small for his hollow eye socket.

"Fishy-fish, fish, fish," the man said. He was almost singing his words in a deep raspy seaman's voice.

His glass eye rolled back and forth, making a click-clack sound, as he leaned over one of the sea women. It was the one that was not yet fully grown, barely post-pubescent by human standards. He pressed his nose to her stomach and smelled her flesh, opening and closing his nostrils rapidly as he inhaled the rotten fish stench.

"My fishy-fish…"

He smiled as he sniffed at her, rubbing the palm of his hand across one of her smooth nippleless breasts. Then he pushed out his tongue, rolled it down her belly toward her lower fish parts. The rancid mucus leaking from her scales only made him lick her more furiously, as if it still contained pheromones that were affecting him. The greasy fluids soaked into his beard, turning his hair from white to a dark grayish green.

"Daddy loves his fishy," he told the corpse, kissing its belly.

As the fisherman caressed and licked the carcass, the odor of rotten fish flooded the room. Even at his distance, the doctor was overpowered by the fishy stink. He felt his stomach trying to curl itself inside out and vomit across the warehouse floor. It was a struggle to keep it down even for someone so accustomed to the smell of decay.

"Daddy wants to be inside of fishy," he said, forcing the end of his beard into his mouth to suck off the fish oils.

The man was absolutely crazed. The doctor could not tell if it was the pheromones that were doing this to him or if it was normal behavior for the man. Either way, Endangered Species Security would have a field day on this guy if they found out what he was doing.

"But fishy needs a hole for daddy," said the fisherman, rubbing his fingers against the fish scales where a human pubic region would have been placed.

He removed his shirt and then grabbed a carving knife from the table. When he pointed the knife at the area where he intended to cut open a new crotch, the doctor realized he couldn't allow this to go any further.

Doctor Black cleared his throat.

The old man froze and looked over at the doctor. Doctor Black just stared back at him calmly, as if not bothered at all by the fact that the man's shirt was off or his mouth was covered in dead mermaid slime.

"Excuse the intrusion, Walt," said the doctor. He believed Walt was the name the old man went by, Doctor Black rarely forgot a name.

"Oh, hello Doctor," said the man, wiping the fish smell on his jeans as if preparing to shake the doctor's hand. He smiled wide, still leaning over the mermaid corpse. He, too, reacted as if nothing was wrong.

The doctor approached the man but they did not shake hands.

"I'm here to autopsy the bodies," said the doctor.

"Do you need any assistance?" he asked, excitedly putting his shirt back on. "I can cut up fish better than anyone in the village. You can even call this place *my* domain."

"Thank you for the offer, but it won't be necessary," said the doctor, noticing the large erection in the man's jeans. "I would prefer to work in privacy."

"Of course," said the old man. His glass eye clicked back and forth as he nodded.

"So if you don't mind..." the doctor said, turning to the bodies.

"Of course..." said the old man.

As the doctor got to work, the old man didn't go right away. He peered over the doctor's shoulder, licking the juice on his whiskers, sniffing at the smell on his fingertips.

The doctor picked up an old rotting fish from the cutting room floor and sliced open its belly to the length of a human vagina. Then he handed it to the fisherman.

"Why don't you go finish yourself off with this," the doctor said. "I can't have you trying to fuck the evidence every time my back is turned."

The old fisherman just frowned at the sliced open fish, as if sticking his dick in a regular fish corpse was just too boring and typical for him. But he took the fish with him as he left the storage room. His erection had no sign of falling any time soon.

Doctor Black had a full hour with the bodies once the old man was gone. After the examination, it was very clear that the wounds on the mermaids' bodies were not caused by a shark attack or attack of another animal of any kind. The holes were created by a man-made tool, something sharp and metal, like the tip of a spear or whaling harpoon. It didn't look good for the people of the village. Somebody there was killing mermaids, and unless an individual stepped forward, the entire community would have to pay the price for it.

CHAPTER FIVE
MUTANT TURTLES

One of the village adolescents had gone missing in the early afternoon. He was the preacher's son, a fourteen-year-old named Adam. The last time he had been seen was when he met up with a group of friends on the cliff overlooking the sea—a common hangout area for the village teenagers.

"Are you sure he didn't go anywhere near the water?" the doctor asked the boy's parents.

The preacher was incredibly muscular, almost twice the doctor's size. He was an older man, closing in on the age of sixty. Even still, he must have been the strongest man in the village. His much younger wife was behind him, tears flooding her dark gray face.

"We're sure," said the preacher. Jim was his name. "Ever since what happened to Edward…" He looked back at his wife. She broke eye contact immediately. "Adam's been terrified to go anywhere near the water."

"Edward was your other son?"

The large man nodded. "He was one of the first victims, a few months back."

"Has Adam been showing any signs of depression?" the doctor asked. "Has he been under a lot of stress?"

The preacher's tone changed from docile to livid. "Are you trying to say my son committed suicide?"

"I'm just trying to eliminate that possibility."

"No son of mine would be such a coward as to kill himself," Jim said, getting in the doctor's face.

"We don't even know he's dead," the doctor said. "He's just missing."

"The boy's dead," Jim yelled. "I've searched everywhere on the island. He was killed by your godforsaken sea demons."

The doctor paused for a moment. He didn't want to argue with the man, not after what he was going through.

"How dangerous are the cliffs?" the doctor asked. "Might he have fallen by accident?"

"Now are you calling my boy a bumbling idiot?" the preacher yelled.

The man looked like he was about to punch the doctor in the face if he said another word. But it was important that the doctor knew the truth. He was dealing with a new species of mermaid, a species that had already proven to discharge much stronger pheromone levels than any species he'd ever encountered. If they were capable of attracting their prey from such a great distance as the boy on the cliff, then the villagers were all in much greater danger than they realized. If only the preacher were more cooperative.

"Have any of the other kids ever bullied your son?" the doctor asked. "Does he have any enemies?"

The preacher stepped forward as if he were going to throw the doctor to the ground, but the sound of the door slamming open stopped him in his tracks.

"Doctor Black," the chief said from the doorway. "Let's go."

"I still have more questions," said the doctor.

"You're finished for now. Jim and his wife need some time alone."

The doctor looked at the fuming preacher. He knew the man wouldn't be much help to him in his state, so he stood up and followed the chief out the door.

"You can't go upsetting my people like that," the chief said to the doctor, as they walked away from the preacher's house.

"They've been through a lot. Jim probably just lost the last of his sons."

"I understand," said the doctor. "But this is important. If it was a mermaid that got him, I have to know exactly how it happened."

"I don't care," said the chief. "You're an outsider here. People don't trust you."

"I have a job to do. They don't need to trust me."

"You're wearing out your welcome far too quickly. You only just arrived last night."

The doctor changed the subject. "I need to borrow a boat."

"What?" Stephen asked, thrown off by the sudden question. "Why do you need a boat?"

"The girl needs to go to Green Rock," said the doctor. "None of your people are willing to take her, so I told her I would do it myself."

"Absolutely not," said the chief. "It's too dangerous. I can't afford to have anything happen to you out there."

"Then I'm not asking you, I'm *telling* you to give me a ship. It'll only be an hour there and back. I'll return by nightfall."

"It's non-negotiable. Our boats are our livelihoods. We don't just lend them to outsiders, even if they aren't in use at the moment."

"What about your father's boat?"

"You're *not* taking my father's boat." Stephen's voice raised to a shout.

"Why not? He's not using it anymore."

Then the chief got into his face and screamed, "You're not taking my father's boat, you motherfucking shit-faced freak."

The chief had the same angry gray expression as the preacher did moments before, glaring at the doctor as if he wanted to kill him. This was not the same pleasant man he had known from previous visits. Old Ethel was right. The young chief was not himself. Something was going on with him.

"That's final," the chief said.

The doctor watched him as he walked away, scratching at an infected wound on the side of his neck.

"That's a long way down," the doctor said to himself.

He stood on the edge of the cliff overlooking the sea, about fifty yards from the chief's secluded mansion. It was the place where the preacher's son had last been seen.

"No way anyone would survive that fall," he said to the waves crashing against the white rocks.

There seemed to be no way for the mermaids to have lured the teenager down using pheromones or even visual stimulation. From the top of the cliff, it was too far to smell or see much of anything below.

"What happened to you Adam?" the doctor asked the wind. "Did you kill yourself? Was life in this drab corner of nowhere too depressing to continue? Or did you just get too close to the edge and slip?"

The doctor wasn't sure how the boy died, but he doubted the mermaids could have seduced him from this distance. Perhaps another kid killed him and wasn't speaking up. With all the disappearances happening every day on the island, a person could easily get away with murder. For all the doctor knew, the preacher himself could have done away with the boy. He could have hit him a little too hard while he was drunk one night and was using the mermaids as a cover story. It probably happened all the time in this village.

As he took a closer look at the rocks below, Black discovered something unusual that he had not noticed on first glance. The rock face was covered in spider webs. Thin, almost invisible webs, that stretched from the top of the cliff all the way down to the crashing waves. These islands were well known for their rare species of spiders that could build whole canopies of webbing in the forest, whole colonies of arachnids working together to build a giant web that even birds would get stuck within. But the doctor had never heard of a web this size, nearly a hundred feet down.

After seeing the web, the doctor knew one thing was certain. The boy didn't fall off this cliff. If he had, he would have disturbed the web, causing it to break apart all the way down the rock face. But the web was completely intact all along the cliff. Something else must have happened to him.

While walking along the cliff edge, the doctor eventually came to the young chief's house. The place was big, too big for a married couple living in such a poor village. It seemed cold and empty in the way that new buildings usually felt. He would have believed the place was deserted if it weren't for the strange woman staring down at him from the second floor window.

The doctor couldn't get a good look at her from the glare on the glass, but he could see her expression was not friendly or inviting. She glowered at him viciously, as if trespassing on her land was incredibly offensive. He understood what Jackson had said about her. The woman must have been mentally ill.

Black just bowed toward the window and turned away. It was getting late in the afternoon and he knew it was about time to help Jackson get to her father's island. He promised to get her there and that was what he would do with or without the chief's help.

Since Doctor Black was staying in the old chief's home, it wasn't difficult to obtain the keys to his boat. He decided to take it without permission. It wasn't as if any of the villagers would chase after him.

"It's not a bad ship," Oswaldo said, as he took the boat out to sea. "Its whiskey reserve is full to the brim." Then he took a swig of liquor.

Doctor Black thought it would be useful taking the old guy along. But seeing how much he was guzzling whiskey while at the controls of the ship, he was beginning to wonder if it wouldn't have been for the best to have left him in the village.

"Thanks again for taking me," Jackson said. "I've tried calling him probably twenty times. There's still no answer."

"We'll be there soon," said the doctor.

Jackson looked up at the cloudy sky. A drizzle of rain sprayed like ice needles on her eyelids. The freezing wind was so strong she couldn't keep her jacket closed.

"You said you want to talk with my father," she said, raising her voice loud enough to speak over the deafening wind. "What's that all about?"

"He's studying the mutations in the area, right?" Black said. "I have reason to believe the mermaids are also mutating."

"Is that why they won't eat your food people anymore?"

The doctor nodded. "Food people are specifically engineered to suit the tastes of each particular species of mimic. If these new mermaids are a mutant species they wouldn't necessarily have the same taste as the old species."

"Mimic? What do you mean by that?"

"It's a classification for animals that attempt to mimic humans," said the doctor. "Mermaids are one of them. But there are also nagas, which are like mermaids but have the lower halves of snakes instead of fish. They have the ability to swallow their victims whole. And arachnians, which have the lower bodies of spiders. And vampires, which are bat-like creatures that drink human blood. All mimics have evolved in such a way so that they can lure their human prey to them."

"Vampires? Seriously?"

"They're much different creatures than the old stories make them out to be. For instance, they are far from immortal. All mimics are on the endangered species list, but vampires are the most endangered of all due to frightened humans trying to wipe them out. They are actually the least dangerous of mimics, because they don't necessarily need to kill their prey in order to feed from them."

"How come nobody talks about any of the other mimics? I've only heard of mermaids."

"Most species of mimics live in secret zoos, where they are protected and preserved. Their existence is not made public. Mermaids are different, though. They are the only mimics who live in the wild, because they do not survive in captivity. It was impossible to keep them a secret from the world for very long."

"And your company provides food for all of these creatures?"

"It's a good business."

"So how are the mermaids mutating?" Jackson asked. "Are they growing eight legs like the turtles my father's studying?"

"No," the doctor said. "They are rapidly evolving to become much stronger hunters than before. They also have fangs, which is leading me to believe that they are becoming vampiric."

"You mean they're vampire mermaids?"

"I mean they're most likely blood-drinkers, which would explain why they didn't have a taste for the food people on the island. The Siren Cove merchow weren't designed for blood drinkers. They hardly have any blood in them at all."

"So all you need to do is get a new type of food people to the island and the villagers will be saved?"

"Most likely," said the doctor. "Although I'm not sure the village is going to be saved even with new food people."

"Why's that?"

"Three mermaids were killed this morning. I'm pretty sure it was the villagers who killed them. Endangered Species Security is going to want their heads for it. If I can't prove the villagers are innocent most of them will probably be transformed into the new batch of food people themselves."

"They'll really do that to them?"

"It's the law."

When they arrived at Green Rock, nobody came out to greet them.

It was a very small island, just large enough for a couple of small buildings and a dock. If it weren't for the unique species of turtles that laid eggs only on this particular beach, the island probably wouldn't have even been put on a map.

"Dad?" Jackson yelled at the buildings, as they pulled up along the dock. She turned to the doctor. "His boat's not here."

She got off the ship and ran down to the beach, yelling for her father. The only sound coming from the houses was the squealing of wind blowing through a cracked window.

Oswaldo tied up the boat as Doctor Black went after the girl. The doctor knew there was a problem right away. It was confirmed when he saw a boat lying on its side beneath the water. It had a large circular hole going through it, just like the one that sank the ship they came in on the day before. It was surely her father's boat.

While following after Jackson, the doctor saw a turtle with eight legs hobbling down the beach toward the water. Its shell was black with red spots. It had six eyes and what looked to be pointed teeth. He had seen pictures of the mutant turtles from this area before, but they were not as odd as this one. The turtles must have mutated even further in only a year's time.

"Dad?" Jackson's voice echoed through the rocks. "Are you here?"

She went through the building that was used as living quarters, but couldn't find her father or his assistant.

Doctor Black went to the other building, the one that was used as a lab. At first, he thought the front entrance to the building was wide open. But once he got to the entryway, he saw that it had been ripped off of its hinges. Lying on the floor, the door was bent and twisted. It had a circular hole in its center, twenty inches wide—the same hole that was in the sunken boat outside.

Jackson came up behind the doctor and gasped when she saw the door on the ground.

"What happened here?" she asked.

The doctor had no idea.

When they entered the lab, there was a sign of a struggle. Tables had been knocked over, equipment smashed against the walls.

"What could have caused this?" Jackson asked. Then she yelled to the next room. "Dad? Are you there?"

She ran into the other room. Then she screamed at the top of her lungs. By the way she screamed, Doctor Black thought she had found her father's dead body. But it wasn't her father's body she found.

When the doctor arrived, he saw a grotesque creature lying on the floor. It was full of bullet holes. It had probably been dead for a few days.

"What is it?" Jackson asked.

The thing was some kind of mutant. It was half man and half fish, but unlike a mermaid it had the upper body of a fish and the lower body of a human. From the waist down, it had human legs and male human genitalia. From the waist up, its fish body was similar to that of a marlin or swordfish. But instead of a sword on its head, this creature had a massive metal drill.

"This might sound crazy," the doctor said, leaning in to touch the dead creature, "but I think this is a merman."

As he touched the corpse, its drill activated, filling the room with a shrill grinding noise. It was a powerful tool, powerful enough to put a hole right through the hull of a ship.

CHAPTER SIX
DRILL FISH

It was incredibly unusual for a species to evolve in such a way, but this merman did somehow grow a large metal drill on its face just as birds grow beaks or moles grow burrowing claws. The most unusual part was how the drill seemed to be powered by gas stored in its digestive tract.

"This thing is a male mermaid?" Jackson cried. "I thought you couldn't tell male and female mermaids apart?"

"This is a new species of mermaid we're dealing with. Their males aren't identical to the females as those previously encountered. Their males are mermen, designed to attract human females."

"How could this thing possibly attract a human female?" she cried. "It's hideous."

"I know it sounds absurd, but look at the size of its sex organ. It is incredibly well-endowed. Yet it is not used for sexual reproduction with mermaids. Its only purpose I can fathom is to attract human female prey."

"That's insane. I could see a lonely sailor mistaking a mermaid for a human woman, but there's no way a woman would mistake this for a man. Especially with that enormous drill-shaped face."

"I believe the mermen developed the drill on their faces not to attract human females, but for a much more useful purpose."

"What could that be?"

"The mermen drill holes in ships in order to sink them. Once the humans abandon ship, the mermaids can pick them off with ease. With the combination of merman and mermaid, this species of mimic is far more dangerous than any previously found in the wild. Not only that, but because they have human legs these mermen are capable of walking on land… at least for short periods of time."

"So this is the creature that sank Oswaldo's boat yesterday?" Jackson asked.

The doctor nodded. Then he looked at the girl with a serious face. He decided to be completely honest with her. The sooner she dealt with the reality of the situation the better.

"And it was also what sunk your father's ship outside," he told her.

She visibly quivered when she heard his words. "What do you mean? My father's ship is gone. He escaped."

The doctor shook his head. "I saw it beneath the water near the dock. It had the same hole drilled through it as the ship did yesterday. I'm sorry."

The girl didn't accept it. She ran out of the building to see for herself.

After taking a moment to study the merman, Doctor Black had a revelation. The wounds on the three mermaids that washed up on the beach that morning could not have been caused by the bites of other mermaids, but they did look like they could have been caused by the drill of a merman.

During the autopsy, the doctor learned that all three mermaid corpses were male. And male mermaids often killed each other when competing for mates. The drill-faced mermen would have no problem dispatching the males of the old species of mermaid.

"Looks like that issue has been resolved," the doctor said.

With this merman corpse and the corpses of the three mermaids, the doctor would have the evidence he needed to prove the villagers innocent of the crime of deliberately murdering an endangered species. Even the assholes at Endangered Species Security would have to accept the proof.

The doctor decided it was time he got in touch with his superiors. Although he still needed to verify a few things, he thought they should know where he was at with the investigation. If Siren Cove needed an entirely new flavor of food people to suit this new species of mermaid, they were going to have to get started right away in order to save the villagers from being continuously preyed upon.

Jackson's father had a satellite phone somewhere on the property. Doctor Black decided to use that one to call his people. But no matter how much he dug through the rubble of the lab, he couldn't find it.

"Maybe the other building…" he said.

He hoped it wasn't in the sunken ship.

As he went for the exit, a phone rang. He turned around. It was definitely in the lab somewhere, out of sight. He followed the sound of the ringing until he returned to the corpse of the merman. It buzzed within his stomach.

Cutting open the cadaver carefully with a scalpel, he removed the contents of the merman's belly. Inside, there was a human hand still intact, severed slightly below the wrist. It was holding the ringing cell phone, clutching it tightly in a death grip.

Although Doctor Black saw the caller's name was listed as *unknown* on the phone's screen, he knew who was calling. It was Jackson, out on the dock, using the chief's satellite phone she had taken without permission. She was desperately trying to get through, praying that her father would answer and tell her that everything was alright.

"Help me with this," Doctor Black said to Oswaldo as he walked out of the lab building, trying to carry the two-hundred-pound

71

merman corpse. The weight of it caused deep indentations in the doctor's clay-like skin.

The drunken boatman didn't help right away, in too much shock at the sight of the creature.

"What in the holy hell is this ugly bastard?" Oswaldo said.

"Just help me," said the doctor. "We need to get out of here. Now."

On board the ship, the doctor took the merman below deck to keep it safe.

"Get us back to Siren Cove as quickly as you can," the doctor told Oswaldo. "Our lives depend on it."

"It's good," Oswaldo said. "No hurry."

"No, it's not good," said the doctor. "Hurry!"

The doctor ran into Jackson as he turned away from the boatman.

"I'm not going back to that place," Jackson said. She was visibly upset.

"You can't stay here," said the doctor. "It isn't safe."

"I don't want to stay here. I want to go back to the mainland to look for my father. You have a boat. You can take me there."

"It's too far away," said the doctor. "We might not make it. There's no telling how many of these mermen are out there. We can't risk being at sea for very long."

"This ship is a lot faster than the piece of crap they sunk yesterday," Jackson said.

"Every minute we're out at sea is a huge risk. I'm not even sure we'll be able to make it to Siren Cove." He waved at Oswaldo to urge him to get moving. "We have to warn the villagers that this species has the ability to move on land. Then if all goes to plan we might just be able to be evacuated by helicopter."

"Who will be picking us up?"

The doctor held up the satellite phone he found in the merman's stomach.

"My people," the doctor said. "I hope…"

"You called them?" Jackson saw the phone he was holding

was her father's, but her brain tried to block it out. She didn't want to admit what she knew was true.

"Yes, but I regret making the call so suddenly, before I had proof," he said. "I thought they would be able to help. Instead, they reported the issue to Endangered Species Security."

"What does that mean?"

"The bastards are on their way here."

"Is that bad?"

"You have no idea," he said. "They are ugly inhuman devils that nobody should ever have the misfortune of meeting. Luckily, I will have the evidence sorted by the time they arrive in Siren Cove."

The doctor decided not to waste any time. He started to dissect the merman on the way to Siren Cove in order to get a better understanding of the species.

"4:45 pm," the doctor said into his digital recording device. "Merman specimen found at the Jackson research camp on Green Rock. The subject had been killed by various gunshot wounds, which appear to have been inflicted in self defense. It is unclear whether Dr. Jackson, his assistant, or an unknown party is responsible."

After examining tissue samples, the doctor said into his recorder, "I have verified that this species is definitely a male mermaid. It is the first true merman on record. Like my previous mermaid encounter, I am unsure whether this is a completely new species of mermaid that invaded the territory from unknown origins or a mutation of the old species."

The doctor dissected the creature's pale-green human penis, trying to figure out what its purpose could be. The results were not what he was expecting.

"The merman species is equipped with what appears to be

human male genitalia. Like the breasts of a mermaid, the tissue is flexible and rubbery like the outer flesh of a jellyfish." The doctor lifted a halved section of testicle below the penis. "I believe the purpose of the faux-genitalia is to act as a kind of stinger, similar to that of a scorpion. It inserts this member into its prey's vaginal cavity where it releases a toxin that would cause paralysis within moments. Judging by the musculature, I believe the organ does not require sexual stimulation in order to extend or inject its poison."

Then the doctor examined one of the only similarities between the male and female of the species. He found them on the creature's waist, between its fish and human divide.

"Like the female subject I encountered, the male has extendable appendages that seem crab-like in appearance. The purpose of these limbs is most likely to hold their prey's upper body into position as their toxin is injected." He went back to the creature's testicle-shaped poison glands. "There appears to be enough venom in reserve so that, if needed, the merman could continue to insert the paralyzing toxin throughout the consumption of its prey."

He moved on from the merman's artificial genitalia and studied its true reproductive organ.

"As I mentioned, the stinger and poison glands have nothing to do with the mating process of the species. Its true reproductive organ is higher up on its abdomen. The organ of this particular specimen appears to be swollen and inflamed. This indicates that it must be the beginning of mating season for the species."

Doctor Black turned off his recording device and contemplated the situation for a moment. He did not know it was mermaid mating season before that moment. Usually, mating season was in late spring or early summer. But this was a new species of mermaid. Their mating season was, evidently, the complete opposite of the old one. They must mate in late fall or early winter.

"This is not good," the doctor said to the merman corpse.

He knew full well that mermaids engage in a feeding frenzy at the beginning of mating season. Without a large herd of specifically engineered food people for the mermaids to gorge themselves on, the villagers of Siren Cove would be in terrible danger.

CHAPTER SEVEN
THE MATING SEASON

There were no signs of mermaids or drill fish, but Doctor Black knew they were in the area as the boat arrived in the harbor at Siren Cove. The faint but distinct scent of honey apricot meant the creatures were nearby, hunting human prey.

"Let's get away from the water as quickly as possible," the doctor told the others. "By twilight, this beach will be swarming with every mermaid in the region."

The doctor pushed Jackson and Oswaldo down the dock, away from the boat. He had to carry the drill fish on his back all by himself, because the drunken boatman had become useless.

"But I didn't tie it up yet," Oswaldo said, turning back toward the boat.

"Forget it," said the doctor, pushing him forward.

He adjusted the fish on his back. It was wrapped in plastic, but the ropes that bound it together were falling apart.

"But I forgot the other bottle of liquor," he said, holding up the mostly empty bottle in his hands.

"We don't have time."

"It's good. I'll just get it real quick."

The doctor could tell that Oswaldo was making up excuses to get closer to the water. The pheromones in the air, though directed at some other victim, were beginning to intoxicate him, allure him. Doctor Black had to get him far away from the beach before it had too strong a hold.

"Just keep moving," the doctor told him, shoving the old man in a straight line away from where he wanted to go.

Jackson wasn't speaking, distraught over her father's disappearance. Doctor Black didn't have time to worry about her.

The whole village was in danger. Still, he was concerned.

"I think you should go back to the house and get some rest," the doctor told her. "I need to find the chief immediately."

The girl nodded at him, but it didn't seem like she actually heard what he had said. He decided to walk her back himself. Oswaldo was also in need of supervision until he was safely indoors.

On the way to the house, they stopped off at the cold storage to drop off the merman corpse. It was important to keep the specimen safe. They couldn't carry it all over town with them. It was vital evidence to prove the villagers were innocent of killing the mermaids.

When they arrived, they carefully placed the drill fish onto one of the cutting room tables. The doctor wanted to leave as quickly as they came, but he stopped in his tracks on the way out. Something in the store room was missing.

"What's wrong with you now?" Oswaldo asked the doctor.

The doctor stared at the three empty tables where the sea women should have been.

"The mermaids," Black said. "They're gone."

"Where'd they go?" asked Oswaldo. "They're dead, right? They can't get up and leave on their own."

"Somebody must have taken them."

The doctor thought of the disturbed old man who was trying to have sex them earlier that day.

"And I think I know exactly who."

He didn't know where Walt lived, but he had to find him and retrieve the mermaids as soon as possible. He did not want to have to explain to ESS why the mermaid corpses were filled with human semen.

"Don't go outside for any reason," the doctor told Jackson and Oswaldo as he dropped them off at the house. "Wait here until I come back. Keep the windows and doors shut."

"Those drill fish men can't reach us here, can they?" Jackson asked. It was the first thing she'd said in a while.

"I don't know yet," said the doctor. "They can definitely walk on land, but for how long I have no idea. Just keep the door closed. The mermen are not the only thing I'm worried about right now."

Jackson wrapped her arms around her stomach. What she really needed at that moment was to pour herself a stiff drink from Oswaldo's bottle.

The doctor had yet to see a single villager since he returned to the island. There were lights emanating from within some of the houses, but no signs of people. He tried the neighbors first, knocking on Cheryl's door. There was no answer.

"Cheryl? Amy?" the doctor yelled. "I'm looking for your brother. Is he around?"

Nobody came to the door.

"Cheryl?"

They didn't appear to be home.

As the doctor stepped away, looking up at the mansion on the cliff above the village, he decided he'd have to make the trek up to the chief's house. There were no lights up there, but it was the most likely place he would find the man.

The cries of a baby filled the air as the doctor started down the road. He turned back. The baby was coming from inside the house.

"Amy?" said the doctor. "Are you home?"

He could only hear the baby crying, but somebody must have been home.

The doctor knocked again. The baby continued to cry inside. He walked around the side of the house. The cries grew louder.

"Amy? Cheryl? Are you home?"

The screen door was open slightly. The doctor slid it open and stepped inside.

"Is your brother around?" he asked.

The baby was in the kitchen. No one else was in sight.

The doctor followed the cries until he saw it. The infant was lying in a deep cooking tray as if it were a crib, sobbing and wiggling its limbs in the air. It wasn't a normal infant. It was a merchow. A baby food person.

The doctor lifted the infant out of the cooking tray. Its dark hollow eyes closed shut, its gaping rotten mouth wide open, and its smoked salmon skin dripping with thick fishy gravy.

"Are you going to be dinner, little one?" the doctor asked.

There were vegetables and potatoes out on the counter. It appeared as if they were basting it like a thanksgiving turkey. The other villagers were eating the food people in order to survive, but he was surprised to see them eating the babies. They didn't have much meat on them.

"Get away from him," said a voice from the doorway.

The doctor looked up and saw the chief's younger sister, Amy, approaching him in her bathrobe. Her gray hair was dripping wet. Her glistening monochrome flesh exposed through the half-opened robe flaps. He couldn't tell if she had just gotten out of the shower or had woken from a nightmare covered in sweat.

"What are you doing to him?" she asked the doctor, taking the baby out of his hands. "Are you trying to cook my baby?"

Her eyes were wide in shock. She had no idea why the infant had been inside the cooking tray.

"I just found him like this. I thought it was rather peculiar myself."

79

She lightly bounced the baby in her arms until it quieted down.

"I wasn't going to eat him," she said. Her tone was different, guilty and defensive. "I was just soaking him in the broth, to give it more flavor."

"Of course," the doctor said.

He realized he was speaking to a mentally ill woman who must be handled delicately. She opened her robe and put the baby to her colorless breast. The infant ravenously sucked at her dark gray nipple.

"I would never hurt my baby," she said.

Doctor Black wasn't sure what to make of her.

"*Your* baby?" the doctor asked. "It's a merchow's infant."

"It's mine," she said, closing the baby up in her robe.

"Did you not take it from one of the female merchows on the beach?"

There were plenty of infants in the herd of food people. The doctor assumed she must have taken one of them. He wondered if she had lost her own child and took one of the livestock to replace it.

"I'm not crazy," she said. "It really is my child. I gave birth to it."

"But it can't be yours. It is a food person."

"It's only half food person," she said.

The doctor looked down at the infant's leg dangling out of her robe. Its flesh was different from that of a normal merchow baby. It was a mixture of smoked salmon and colorless monochrome human flesh. It was half human.

"You mean..." the doctor began.

She broke eye contact.

"Interesting," the doctor said.

"You don't understand," she said. "It gets lonely here. All the men are either dead or married already. I just needed someone to hold. Somebody to keep my bed warm."

"You took a food person into your bed?" he asked.

"I wasn't planning on having sex with him. It just sort of happened. I only wanted a warm body to curl around me. But when I took my clothes off, and we were under the covers together..."

The doctor rolled his eyes at her. "That was a mistake. Food people are designed to be sexually aggressive."

"I don't regret it," she said. "It was nice... When the lights were off, and we were together, it was like I had a real boyfriend. A human boyfriend." Then she looked away and shook her head. "I was so lonely..."

"And you became pregnant?" asked the doctor.

He had never heard of a hybrid between human and food person before. It was possible, of course, but he never could have thought it would ever happen.

She nodded her head. "When my father found out, he wouldn't let me near the beach again. He almost wouldn't let me keep my baby, but I convinced him I'd give it up when it got older." She looked down on it and smiled. "I don't know... I love him so much. I don't think I could ever let the mermaids have him."

The doctor thought it was as interesting as it was disgusting, but he didn't have any more time to waste. He had other business to attend to.

"I'm looking for your brother," the doctor said. "I need to talk to him."

She pointed out of the screen door to the top of the hill.

"He's with the other fishermen," she said. "I think they're looking for the missing boy."

The doctor looked out toward the hill. It was now completely dark out. There were no signs of flashlights or the sounds of ATVs up there. It was just as quiet as the rest of the island.

"Are you sure they're up there?" he asked.

She shrugged her shoulders and smiled her wide gray lips at the crispy creature wiggling in her arms.

All of the houses along the dirt roads on the way up the hill were just as quiet as the rest of the neighborhood. Nobody seemed to be inside of any of them. One house even had its door left open, the wind slamming it against its frame almost angrily. Everyone must have been searching the island for the teenager or they were asleep in their beds.

As the doctor went through the neighborhood, some movement caught his attention. Something in the bushes was thrashing and shaking. It was on the side of the abandoned house he had seen earlier in the day, when he ran into the deformed boy.

The bushes thrashed even more when the doctor came close. Something was in there, growling and grunting. He couldn't see what it was, but it sounded mostly human. It sounded like the boy. Something was wrong with him.

"Are you okay in there?" the doctor asked the quaking bushes.

The boy, if it was the boy, did not respond. The growling sounds became more wild and fierce. The doctor was beginning to think the boy was trapped in there, tangled up in the weeds and thrashing desperately to get free.

"Do you need help?" he asked.

The sounds continued.

The doctor debated going in after the boy but ultimately decided to move on. He wasn't sure if it was the boy or a wild animal. Either way, he didn't have time to stop. So he walked away, leaving the neighborhood for the woods.

Up ahead, hidden through the trees near the top of the cliff, there was a bonfire. It must have been where all the villagers had gone off to, though Doctor Black still didn't see any other signs of human life.

When he stepped through the trees, there were only three men there, watching the fire. It was Stephen the chief, Jim the preacher, and Walt the fisherman with the long white beard. They just stood there with their arms crossed, not saying a word.

"Chief, we need to talk," the doctor said as he stepped out of the trees.

When the chief saw him, a look of surprise hit his face. Then he blocked the doctor's way to the fire.

"You took the boat without permission," the chief said. His tone was deep and annoyed. He sounded like he'd been drinking all day.

"It doesn't matter," the doctor said. "We've got trouble coming. The village isn't safe."

"Why is that?" the chief asked. Then he took a swig of cheap blended whiskey from a quart-sized canteen.

"The reason your mermaids aren't eating your livestock is because they aren't the same mermaids," said the doctor. "These mermaids are stronger, more brutal creatures. They have the ability to lure men in from much farther inland."

The doctor glanced at the fire behind them. For a second, it looked as if the fire was filled with dead bodies.

"Not only that, but the male of the species has the ability to walk on land," he continued. "They're incredibly dangerous." The chief and the old man snickered at him, as if they were too drunk to believe him. "I found one in Dr. Jackson's camp at Green Rock."

The preacher came toward the doctor, towering over him with his arms crossed. He just stared down at him, but didn't react. As if he weren't even listening.

"I believe it was these mermen that killed the mermaids that washed up on the beach this morning," said the doctor. "Your people will not be blamed for the incident. Once I re-examine the bodies I'm sure the results will show that you're innocent."

83

"That's something I wanted to talk to you about," said the chief. "You know those bodies that we found?" He took a swig and then shook his head. "We never found them."

The doctor's eyebrows curled with confusion.

"What do you mean by that?"

The chief chuckled. "We're not going to let you report what happened. As far as you're concerned, you saw nothing."

The doctor still didn't understand until he looked more carefully at the fire behind them. Inside the pit, there were three burning bodies. They were the corpses of the mermaids. It wasn't the creepy old man who stole their bodies. The chief had taken them to get rid of the evidence.

"You idiots..." the doctor said, his eyes widening at the flaming fish women. "You have no idea what you've done."

"It's the only thing we could do," said the chief. "You left us with no other option."

"But I could have proven you were innocent if you didn't burn the evidence."

"It doesn't matter. You can't report this now. You have no choice but to keep it a secret."

"It's too late to keep it a secret," said the doctor.

"Do you know how many dead mermaids wash up on the beach each year?" asked the chief. "It happens all the time. They get attacked by sharks, hit by boats, get sick, get old. They die all the time for all kinds of reasons. And we've never reported any of their deaths. There are dead mermaids buried all over this island."

"You don't understand," said the doctor.

The chief poked his index finger into the doctor's chest. "No, *you* don't understand." He raised his voice to a yelling tone. "You don't know what it's like living here, terrified of being killed by those fucking monsters out there. And if you're lucky to live long enough to have a family, you'll be rewarded by getting to see at least one of your children murdered by those sea bitches." His finger poked the doctor again, squishing a hole into his clay-like flesh. "But the worst of it is everyone else in the world cares more about the mermaids than they do about us. They go to great lengths to protect the mermaids. But who's going to protect us? We aren't even allowed to defend ourselves."

"That is why my company provides you with food people," said the doctor, "so that you don't have to live in danger."

"Fuck your food people," said the chief. "A hell of a lot of good they've done for us."

The chief stepped away, looking back at the bonfire. The preacher, Jim, took a long swig of a liquor bottle. Doctor Black understood what was going on. They had been mourning the loss of the teenage boy out there in the woods. That's why they burned the mermaids. That's why they were drinking.

"If you actually give a shit about my people then you won't report what happened," said the chief. "Don't tell them you ever saw the mermaids. Then there won't have to be any investigation. We'll all be safe. Not just my people, but you and your family as well."

The doctor removed his hat from his head, not sure how to tell him the truth.

"You don't understand," the doctor said. "I already reported the incident to my superiors."

The chief looked over at him with venom in his eyes. "What did you say?"

"I had proof of your innocence," said the doctor. "If you just would have kept the bodies in the cold storage everything would have been fine."

"You told them about the dead fish…"

The doctor nodded. "The ESS is on its way here to investigate it now. They weren't happy about what happened at all. It's going to take a lot to explain it to them, especially after what you've done."

The chief just stood there, glaring at the doctor. He realized the situation he had just put himself in, but it was the doctor he blamed for all of this.

Then he charged him.

"You motherfucker," the chief yelled.

He punched the doctor in the face. His gloved hand made a fist-shaped imprint in his cheek.

"You've killed us!" The chief punched him again, flattening his nose against his face.

"Not necessarily," said the doctor, his voice muffled and nasally from the smashed nose. "I might still be able to prove your innocence."

"Bullshit!" said the chief, punching a hole in his stomach. "Those ESS bastards don't give a shit about our innocence."

The doctor tried to run away, but the preacher grabbed him and held him in place as the chief punched him again. Walt giggled and jumped up and down, blowing the smell of rotten fish in his direction.

"Those fuckers are going to die," said the chief, caving in another section of the doctor's face. "They step foot on my island and I'll feed their asses to the sea bitches myself. See how they like it."

Then they took turns beating the doctor. They didn't care about whether he deserved such a beating or not. They just needed a punching bag and he was the perfect man for the job.

When they brought him back, the doctor's body was twisted and distorted. His face was a lumpy mess. They took him into a warehouse behind the old chief's house, full of ancient fishing supplies. They opened up a cellar door and kicked him down the steps into the darkness.

Lying on the cold muddy ground, the doctor wheezed at them, choking on his words. "You don't understand the danger you're in. You're not safe. It's mating season."

The drunken fishermen weren't listening.

"You can rot down there until we figure out what to do with you," said the chief.

"It's mating season," the doctor tried to yell.

But they didn't listen as they shut him in the shadows.

When they returned twenty minutes later, Jackson and the boatman were with them. They tossed the old drunk down the steps but let Jackson walk down on her own.

"What's going on?" she asked them.

But they didn't respond. They just shut the door on her and left her in the dark.

The doctor pulled out his flashlight so that Jackson could see her way down the steps. She felt her pockets as she stepped down one step at a time, looking for the satellite phone she had stolen from the chief. It wasn't on her.

"Damn grays," Oswaldo said, rubbing his bruised forehead and trying to stand up. "Horrible, horrible people I've always said."

Jackson screamed when she saw the doctor's face. He looked like a mutant creature with his face so bent and misshapen.

"What happened?" Jackson asked.

"I told the chief that ESS was on its way," said the doctor. His voice was just as distorted as his face. "He wasn't too happy about that."

"So he deformed you and threw us all down here?"

She walked toward the doctor, looking around the cellar. The place was as large as the warehouse above it, but cluttered with all kinds of junk. Most of the stuff was ancient fishing supplies, mud-caked and covered in fish oil residue. It probably all belonged to the chief's great grandfather. These small fishing communities never threw anything away.

"He's scared. He burned the dead mermaids while we were gone. Now the ESS will obviously think he's covering it up."

"Are they that scary?" Jackson asked, sitting down next to the doctor to examine his freakish wounds. "Endangered Species Security?"

The doctor nodded. "They aren't human. They're monsters. The chief is right to fear them." He looked at himself in a metal surface to see just how bad his face was. Then he continued, "The ESS believes humans and animals should be equal. They believe they should have equal rights. Basically, if you murder an animal they think you should receive the death penalty just as you would for killing another human being."

"It's a good thing they don't make the laws."

"But when it comes to an endangered species, they actually can make the laws. They have complete power to protect endangered species at any cost. Even human rights mean nothing when it comes to protecting these animals. That's why the mermaid laws are so harsh."

"They'd rather have humans die than mermaids?"

"Definitely. They care far more for the mermaids than the humans that are preyed upon. In fact, the ESS was the main group trying to get food people banned. Not because they thought it was inhumane to transform prisoners into feeder food, but because they thought the food people were unhealthy for mermaids. They thought real humans would be more nutritious, claiming the food people to be full of chemicals and preservatives."

"What the fuck?" Jackson cried.

"They wanted the mermaids to keep eating fishermen or be fed non-modified human livestock."

"And those people are coming here?"

The doctor nodded. "Hopefully we'll still be locked down here when they arrive. If we're being held prisoner they'll know without a doubt that we're not involved with the villagers."

"The whole thing is just ridiculous," Jackson said. "They're just fish."

"Don't say anything like that when the ESS arrives," said the doctor. "To them, you're just a human."

Oswaldo was searching the cellar for some alcohol. He insisted there had to be a case of wine down there somewhere.

"These fishing villages have liquor stashed everywhere," said the boatman. "I'll find some within the hour. I promise you."

Doctor Black was busy remolding his face back to its original shape.

"How are you able to do that?" Jackson asked. "It seems like it would be impossible to get your face back to normal."

"It won't go exactly back to normal," said the doctor. "This happens to me all the time. I have to sculpt my face every morning."

"So you can completely change your facial features if you want?"

"I try to mold the same face every day, but I probably never get it right. My face always looks a little off."

As the boatman wandered into the dark corners of the room, he yelled back at the others, "Hey, there's something over here."

The doctor looked at him, wondering if he actually found the liquor he was searching for.

"It's moving," said the boatman.

Then a figure came out of the shadows. It stepped slowly at first, then it charged forward. Oswaldo screamed.

"It's coming!" the boatman cried.

The creature hissed as it ran. When the doctor saw it, he couldn't believe his eyes. He knew exactly what it was.

"Get down," the doctor yelled, grabbing a crowbar from a

junk pile. "Cover your face."

The creature was a rabid merchow. Large bubble-shaped skin sacks grew from its chest and shoulders. Unlike the other food people, it had human eyes, long gray hair and a beard.

The doctor charged it with the crowbar, but before he could reach it, the bubbles on the merchow's chest exploded. Black spores sprayed into the air, covering the boatman's back and face.

"Duck!" the doctor yelled at the drunk.

Oswaldo dropped to his knees as the doctor swung the crowbar at the creature's face. The merchow's skull popped open as easily as a ball of popcorn. Powdery fish-like flesh exploded into a fuzzy black cloud, drizzling down on them like ash. The food person went limp and fell to the ground, its body curling up like a dead spider among the refuse.

As Doctor Black caught his breath, Jackson came to him.

"What the hell was that?" she asked.

The doctor pushed her out of the way and went to the boatman.

"It looked like a food person," she said.

The doctor wiped the spores off of the boatman's face as quickly as he could.

"It *was* a food person," said the doctor. Then he pointed at the creature's face. It was that of an old monochrome man. "It was also the old chief of Siren Cove. Stephen's father."

The doctor used rags and scraps of plastic, trying to get all of the black powder off of Oswaldo's skin.

"I don't get it," Jackson said. "How did Stephen's father become a merchow?"

"Through infection," the doctor said, helping the boatman to his feet. "You see those spore sacks on the thing's body?"

He pointed to the merchow corpse. "Those spores can turn humans into food people."

"What…" Jackson stepped away from Oswaldo who was covered in the spores.

"I've never seen the disease outside of the lab," said the doctor. "It's incredibly contagious. It causes food people to become violent and rabid." The doctor covered the merchow body in a plastic tarp. "Stephen must have locked his father down here after he got the disease. Either that, or the old chief locked himself down here so that he wouldn't infect anyone else."

The doctor sat the boatman down away from the merchow corpse. "What bugs me is why none of the livestock showed any sign of this infection or why the chief didn't mention it to me."

"Maybe the villagers killed off the infected ones before you arrived," Jackson said.

"Perhaps," the doctor said. "Let's just hope the food people that the villagers were eating weren't the infected ones. Otherwise, the majority of the community would be contaminated."

Jackson pointed at the boatman. He was curled up in the corner.

"What about him?" she asked. "Is he going to be okay?"

The doctor went to the boatman.

"Are you alright?" the doctor asked him.

"My fingers are tingling like the devil," said the drunkard.

"You need to get all of this off of your skin," he said to Oswaldo, pointing at the black spores. "It's incredibly hazardous."

The drunk nodded and continued wiping his limbs.

Jackson and the doctor stayed away from him.

"Is he infected?" Jackson asked.

"Most likely," said the doctor. "But he can be cured if we get him back to the mainland in time."

The doctor hoped the ESS would be willing to help them

when they arrived. Otherwise, Oswaldo would be dead. Perhaps they all would be dead.

Doctor Black's fingers burrowed through his flesh like earthworms in mud. He was sculpting his face back to its original form. His nose smoothed into an arch, his eyebrows squished into ridges, his lips pinched into puffy mounds. Now he was working on his ears. He always had the most difficulty with the ears.

Jackson watched, amazed by how quickly he was able to mold himself back together. She found it grotesque yet fascinating and almost beautiful. The doctor had turned his diseased flesh into an art form.

"It really is like clay," Jackson said.

They were both on the other side of the cellar, sitting away from the boatman and the diseased corpse. Oswaldo was curled up in the corner, fast sleep. It was the best thing for him to do. Sleep would slow the infection.

"That's why the disease will soon kill me," the doctor said, curling his fingers into his ears. "You can't survive long with clay flesh. At first, it was just the outer layer of skin that was soft and pliable. But then it went deeper. Now, even my internal organs are like clay. Within days, my heart will be completely transformed and won't be strong enough to pump blood through my body."

The doctor removed his clothes, stripping down to his underwear. His body was covered in lumps and fist-shaped craters. He smoothed down his chest and sculpted the skin around his muscles.

"Why do you bother putting so much effort into putting yourself back together so perfectly? You're inevitably going to fall apart again whenever someone bumps into you or you sleep face-down on a pillow."

The doctor tried remolding the misshapen sections of his back, but was having difficulty reaching them.

"I must be presentable," he said, just barely scooping at his deformed shoulder blade with his index finger. "Why clean your house every day if it's only going to eventually become a mess? Plus, I'd rather die a man than a shapeless blob."

Jackson couldn't bear to watch him struggle so much to reach his back. She kneeled down behind him and placed her gloved hands on his shoulders.

"What are you doing?" he asked. "You can't touch me."

"I have gloves on," she said. "Let me do it."

She squeezed his shoulders, digging her fingers into his flesh, just to see what it would feel like. It felt less like clay than she imagined. It still had the warmth of human flesh, the same texture and appearance. It wasn't as breakable as clay. It was just as firm as human flesh but could be moved and reshaped.

"I once watched an erotic film where two people with Zimmer's made love," Jackson said.

She rubbed the palm of her hand up his spine, pushing a mound of flesh up his back like a bulldozer.

"They molded their skin together, smoothing the cracks between them." A smile was on her face as she moved her fingers through his skin. "You couldn't tell one from the other. I don't know why, but I always thought it was incredibly sexy."

After she finished molding his back, she didn't want to stop. She continued stroking his muscles, sculpting deep curves.

"It's a horrible disease," said the doctor. "There's nothing sexy about it."

The girl stuck her finger into his flesh, in the center of his back.

"You said you'd rather die a man than a shapeless blob," Jackson said, looking at the hole in his flesh she just created. "But why not die a work of art?"

She carved a circle around the hole. Then a circle around

that circle. She created a spiral in his flesh, moving outward across his back.

"What are you doing to me?"

"Close your eyes," she said, rubbing her fingertip through his skin. "Think of it as a massage."

The doctor responded by exhaling all the air out of his lungs. What she was doing did not seem appropriate to him, but it did feel soothing. He closed his eyes and allowed her to draw on him.

"Your flesh is like a zen garden," Jackson said. "I'm using my finger as a rake to dig spiral patterns through your flesh like zen garden sand."

The doctor didn't respond. He inhaled deeply as her finger moved toward the edges of his ribs. When she could not go any further, she poked a hole on his shoulder and spiraled out from there. Then she etched his chest.

After a couple of hours, the doctor's body was covered in spiral patterns. It looked like a giant had pressed a thumb against his body, leaving behind an enormous fingerprint across his skin.

"You look beautiful," Jackson said. "Now you're a work of art."

The doctor didn't say anything, blinking slowly as if he had just come out of a trance. He looked at his arms in the dimness of the flashlight. The deep canals carved in his flesh created shadows, giving it the appearance of black spirals tattooed into his flesh.

When he looked down at his underwear, Doctor Black saw that he had an erection. He hadn't realized it until that moment. At first he thought it was because of the woman's strangely intimate touch, but then he realized it was something else. The smell of honey apricot was getting strong in the air. He was breathing in mermaid pheromones, causing him to become intensely aroused.

"I can't believe it," the doctor said. "I can smell them."

Jackson sniffed at the air, wondering what he was talking about.

"We're almost a kilometer from the shore and sealed underground," said the doctor. "If the mermaid pheromones can reach us all the way here then no one in the village above is safe."

CHAPTER EIGHT
ENDANGERED SPECIES

The doctor took the last of his pills to clear his head. The mermaid pheromones had been making him dizzy. He could hardly think straight and his erection was becoming bothersome.

"What do we do?" Jackson asked.

"This is probably the safest place we could be on this island right now," said the doctor. "The mermaids kill by luring their prey to them. It's impossible to lure us if we're locked down here."

The boatman tossed and thrashed in his sleep. The pheromones were affecting him, making him sexually ravenous.

"What will happen to the villagers?"

"The women outnumber the men up there," said the doctor. "They might be able to hold them back or restrain them."

"Can't we do something to help them?"

The boatman awoke and staggered up the stairs toward the door. He was deliriously intoxicated by both alcohol and mermaid pheromones. When the cellar hatch wouldn't open normally, he shook the handles. Then he banged his shoulder into it, drool oozing down his beard.

"Get away from there," the doctor told him, stepping toward the old man.

He slammed himself into the door, banging on it, trying to get out.

"That door is reinforced," the doctor said. "You can't possibly get through it."

But that only made the boatman slam into the door harder, harder.

"Let me out," the boatman cried. "I need out."

"You're only going to hurt yourself," said the doctor.

The boatman began ranting deliriously in Portuguese. He rattled the door, pounding his knuckles against the wood until they became bloody. The pheromones made him wild. His erection poked out the top of his sagging pants.

The doctor went up the steps toward him, shining the flashlight on his back.

"Don't you realize what you're doing?" the doctor asked.

The boatman didn't care about the danger. He wanted and needed to be the mermaid's prey. The doctor knew he had to restrain him.

"Get away from there," the doctor said, pulling the boatman away from the door.

When the boatman was pulled back, he turned to the doctor and shrieked. The doctor let go of him the second he saw what was wrong. It wasn't just the pheromones that were affecting him. The spore infection was spreading through his skin. The entire right side of his face was the texture of smoked salmon. The life in one eye had faded out. He was already half food person.

"Get away from me!" the boatman cried, his voice vicious and rabid.

Then he threw the doctor down the stairs and went back to pounding on the door. The steps put three large dents in the doctor's newly reshaped flesh on the way down.

"Don't go near him," the doctor said, as Jackson helped him to his feet. "He's already transforming."

Jackson looked at the crazed man. He was now scratching violently at the door, as if trying to dig through it. His fingernails cracked open and bent backwards like peeling skin from garlic. A trail of blood smeared down the wood as the flesh on his fingers and knuckles was stripped away. "Are we just going to let him keep going?" Jackson said.

"He won't be able to get through," said the doctor.

The door was completely red with blood.

"But look what he's doing to himself," she said.

"He's a dead man anyway," the doctor said. "The infection spread too quickly. I've never seen anything like it. He's beyond help."

The doctor went through the junk in the cellar, looking for something he could use as a weapon.

"What are you doing?" Jackson said.

"Catch." He tossed her the crowbar he used to kill the food person with. She caught it, but it caused a hammering pain when it collided with a bone in her palm. "We need to be able to defend ourselves just in case he turns."

Jackson saw the boatman was becoming more crazed by the minute. He was humping the door, rubbing his erection into the wood, slamming his face until his nose split open.

The doctor returned carrying an old iron trident. Jackson did a double-take when she saw it. She wondered if the fishing village actually once used tridents to fish.

"I've never seen anyone so affected by the pheromones before," the doctor said. "Not only are the mermaids dangerous, but their prey are also dangerous if you get in their path. I bet he would claw his way through his own mother if she stood in place of the door."

The flesh on the boatman's fingertips had been torn away until there were only nubs of bone, creating a high-pitched squeal as they scraped across the hatch. He kept scratching, grinding his finger bones into the wood, leaving a powder residue as they were shaved down like chalk on a blackboard.

"Get ready," the doctor said. "He'll turn on us at any minute."

Jackson could tell that the boatman was more merchow than human now. He slammed against the meat-coated door, thrashing with unnatural strength. There was a loud cracking noise, then another crack. The boatman's ribs were breaking as he rammed his body into the hatch.

"He's really not giving up," Jackson said. "Even though it's going to kill him."

When the boatman slammed one last time, there was an even louder crack. But this time it wasn't his bones. It was the door. He rammed into the door again, then again, and finally broke through.

The mangled half food man screamed in ecstasy, charging out of the cellar and through the warehouse, leaving a trail of gore behind.

The doctor and Jackson just looked at each other. Then they went up the steps, out of the cellar.

They saw the boatman run out of the warehouse, disappearing into a thick fog that had swallowed the town.

Carrying the trident like a walking stick, the doctor stepped out of the warehouse, listening carefully. The smell of honey apricot was even stronger in the open. He contemplated locking himself back inside the cellar.

"Let's see who's still around," the doctor said.

Jackson nodded, holding the crowbar up like a baseball bat.

They walked slowly onto the main road of the village, unable to see more than twenty feet in the fog. The village was still and quiet. There was a cracking sound in the distance, a toppling of a garbage can, and a stray gunshot high in the hills, but for the most part the place was dead silent.

"Let's try next door first," the doctor said, leading them toward Cheryl and Amy's house.

There were no lights inside the house. There were no lights coming from any of the homes on the block. Just a few street lights reflecting against the fog.

"Cheryl?" the doctor asked. "Amy?"

But he didn't need to call their names. Their door was broken down. Nobody was in there.

Jackson looked around at the doors of other homes surrounding them. They were all torn down. They had large circular holes through them.

"Drill fish…" Jackson said.

The doctor looked down at the broken door and grunted in agreement.

"They're able to come this far inland," he said. "If there were villagers in these houses they didn't stand a chance."

"How many of them are there do you think?" Jackson asked.

The doctor went across the street and looked at the damaged houses one by one. Their windows were smashed in, doors torn down, even walls had holes in them.

"A whole army," the doctor said.

Then he tightened his grip on the trident in his hands and tried to shake the pheromones as they tightened their grip on his brain.

The silence was broken by a scream. It was coming from down the road. A man crying for help.

"Let's go," the doctor said, charging down in the direction of the shouts.

Doctor Black was surprised to hear someone screaming. The victims of mermaids never cried for help. They were always too drugged to cry, too entranced to realize they were in danger.

They followed the sound of the man's cries until they came to the fence separating the beach and the harbor from the town.

It was Jim, the preacher. The giant man was lying on the ground, holding onto the fence for dear life, bawling like a baby. He was also wearing an odd homemade gasmask, which seemed to have been blocking out the pheromones.

"Help me!" he shrieked when he saw the doctor and Jackson approaching.

They came toward him. Most of his lower body was covered

in fog, but they could tell something had a hold of him, trying to pull him toward the water. The fence he was gripping had been shredded apart by a dozen giant drills. All he was holding onto was a chain-link flap that unraveled in his hands.

"Don't worry," the doctor said as he approached him. "I'll get you out of here."

The preacher's eyes were so full of shock that the doctor wasn't sure he'd even heard him. When the doctor tried to see what was pulling on the preacher, he noticed that the large man had been bound. He was wrapped in wires, almost cocooned by them. The doctor had never seen anything like it.

"They're inside me," the preacher screamed.

By the time the doctor reached for the man's hands, his fingers slipped free. The preacher screamed as he was dragged through the sand away from them. His gasmask fell from his face, a geyser of blood erupting from his mouth.

"What the hell was that?" Jackson cried.

The doctor didn't answer. He reached through the fence and retrieved the gasmask the preacher was wearing. It was old. It looked as if it were something the villagers used a long time ago, before the food people or hormone pills, to protect themselves from the mermaid pheromones.

"Put this on," the doctor said. "Just in case the pheromones can also affect you."

If she was already affected by the pheromones she would have already shown signs of intoxication by now. But the doctor didn't know if the mermen released similar spellbinding toxins to lure their female victims. He thought it would be better to stay on the safe side.

"It's covered in blood," Jackson said, holding it away from her.

Hissing noises came from the fog. The doctor looked around, wondering what was causing them. There was also a loud rustling sound, like clothes on a clothesline rippling through the wind.

"Just put it on," he told her.

She wiped off the blood and pulled it over her face, as the hissing noises closed in on them.

From out of the fog, smoky black bodies ran toward them. They were infected food people, hissing and gnashing, foaming at the mouth like rabid beasts. Spore sacks grew from their necks and shoulders. Eyes glared red with ferocity.

"Run," the doctor yelled.

They went in the other direction, up the hill, but only ran into more food people. The chewy-fleshed creatures were stepping out of blue and purple homes with deranged looks in their eyes. All of them had once been villagers. They must have transformed from eating infected meat. Jackson and the doctor found themselves surrounded.

"There's too many," Jackson yelled, her voice muffled beneath the gasmask.

"Their skulls are soft," said the doctor. "Take them down before they release their spores."

The doctor ran at a snarling food woman and pierced her skull with his three-pronged spear. It took a moment to realize she was Ethel, the village elder. The old woman wasn't immortal after all. As Ethel died she grabbed the shaft of the trident and released a black cloud of spores. The doctor was far enough away to avoid most of them, but Jackson ran right through the cloud on her way to swing her crowbar at another food person's skull. He hoped the gasmask on her face would be protection enough.

Jackson smashed at the food people wildly as they surrounded her, breaking one of their arms and blinding another, but she didn't land any killing blows. One of them grabbed her around the throat and hissed at her like a skinless cat. She lowered her crowbar through its face, ripping a crater into its head where the nose and mouth used to be. But the creature didn't die. The spore sacks on its body exploded into her face.

"Hurry," the doctor cried, slashing two of the food people through their necks.

As she tried to wipe away the soot covering her gasmask, the doctor grabbed her by the shoulder and pulled her along. They ran up the hill, away from the bright pink and purple homes. The ravenous creatures came after them. A child led the pack. It was the same child with the deformed face the doctor had met earlier in the day. Doctor Black now understood where the boy's deformities had come from. He had been transforming into a merchow since early that morning.

"Get to the chief's house," the doctor yelled as they ran. "It's bound to be the safest place on the island."

"But that guy wants to kill you," she said, quickly running out of breath as they went up the steep slope.

"I'm sure he's come to his senses by now," said the doctor. "After everything that's happened to his village, he'll need all the help he can get."

The food people didn't follow them all the way up the hill. Halfway there, they seemed to lose interest and turn around, as if something had scared them off.

"There it is," Jackson said, as they saw the mansion at the end of the dirt road.

"The lights are on," said the doctor. "At least it's a sign that somebody could still be there."

As they came closer to the house, they could tell something was not quite right with the place. There were shiny wires covering the trees and windows, the same as the ones wrapped around the preacher as he was dragged away.

"What the hell are those?" Jackson asked, pointing at things that moved in the distance.

There were giant spider-like creatures coming up from the cliffs behind the house, climbing across the side of the building. Just a few of them, moving slowly like shadows. When the doctor understood what they were, his eyes widened. He couldn't believe it, but it was true.

"They're mermaids..." the doctor said.

He moved in for a closer look. The three creatures walking along the side of the building were really mermaids.

"How can they possibly be mermaids?" Jackson said, staying close behind the doctor. "They're walking on land."

"Remember when I said that this new species was vampiric?"

Jackson nodded, not sure where he was going.

"The fangs threw me off," the doctor said. "I thought the mermaids had evolved to become more like vampires, but it wasn't vampires. They've mutated into arachnians."

"Arachnians?"

"The spider mimics."

The doctor examined the creatures more carefully. The crab-like appendages that extended out of the mermaids' shoulders were not the only ones. They also had six much larger limbs that came out of their lower fish bodies, enabling them to walk on land.

The spider mermaids crawled across the roof of the house, leaving thick thread-like wires that grew from the lower half of their fishtails. They created a network of webs outside the house to trap the prey that hid within. It was the same webbing that the doctor had found covering the cliffs earlier in the day.

"Let's go," the doctor said.

"Where are we going?"

"Inside," said the doctor, as he went toward the mansion.

"Are you fucking with me?" Jackson said, yanking on his arm. "That place isn't safe."

"We have to help the people within," said the doctor.

Then he charged for the entrance, ducking under spider webs and trying not to inhale too much of the air thick with pheromones.

When the doctor burst through the front door of the chief's mansion, he ran into something he was not at all expecting—music. The halls echoed with classical violin music playing on a distant record. The room was wide and empty. The lighting dim. The fact that nobody was around made the music all the more haunting.

Jackson came in behind him and closed the door. She went to remove the gasmask from her face but the doctor told her to keep it on. He didn't think it was safe to remove yet.

"Somebody's here, right?" she asked. "Somebody's got to be."

They stepped forward. There were no signs of an attack, but there was almost an inch of water on the floor. The water was stagnant and mold grew along the walls. It looked as though the house had been flooded for a long time and nobody bothered to clean it up.

"Amy?" the doctor said, as he saw a woman sitting on a couch in one corner.

The chief's sister was in a daze. She was topless, breast-feeding her merchow baby. She didn't respond, staring off into space. As the doctor approached, he saw what was wrong. The woman was infected by the food people disease. Half her face and shoulders were transformed into smoked salmon skin, including the breast her baby suckled. She was becoming the same species as her hybrid child.

As Jackson went toward her, the doctor held her back.

"Leave her," he said. "She's already gone."

Around the corner, there was a massive aquarium that took

105

up much of the room. It was dark and filled with scum. A crack down the glass caused it to leak all over the floor. For a second, the doctor wondered what the chief was keeping inside of the thing. But then he saw what it was, coming toward him.

Wrapped in the chief's arms, it flowed into the room, across the sopping floor. To the violin ballroom music, they danced, embracing one another.

"What is going on?" Jackson said.

She couldn't believe her eyes. Nor could the doctor, who had never seen anything like it in all of his life. The chief was dancing with a mermaid. His eyes locked into hers, drifting in and out of trance. Her crab appendages gently hugging his neck. Her spider legs tapping across the floor like high-heeled tango shoes. Somehow, the chief had her trained.

"That's her," Jackson said, pointed at the woman. "That's the creepy woman I saw in the window. It's his wife."

The doctor had no idea how they were dancing together. Mermaids are just fish. Nothing more. But there she was, wearing an elegant dress that covered the top half of her body. Her fishtail and spider legs hung out the bottom. It was unnatural. The predator showed no desire to attack her prey.

"Aren't they beautiful?" said a voice from behind.

They turned, but saw no one.

"They are so in love," the voice continued.

The doctor couldn't find who was speaking until he looked up. Covering the ceiling was a massive spider web, created by the chief's mermaid. Several dead bodies were cocooned in the web, monochrome husks dangling from threads. The latest victim was only recently cocooned in the web. It was the chief's older sister, Cheryl.

"Look at how gracefully she moves," Cheryl said.

The doctor stepped toward her and looked up at the ceiling. The woman hung upside-down, facing him.

"Your brother did this to you?" the doctor asked.

The chief must have been feeding his own villagers to this

mermaid spider for weeks. It was detestable, insane. The doctor couldn't believe a man who was so fervent to save his people would do such a thing.

"It's not his fault," Cheryl said. "Whenever he's around her, he becomes someone else. She drives him mad with passion. He'll do anything to make her happy."

The chief and the mermaid seemed to not realize anyone was in the room with them, wrapped up in their own magical world.

"It's a fairy tale come true," Cheryl said. "Just like in The Little Mermaid."

Then the sound of drills erupted from the walls around them.

"Get back," the doctor said, pushing Jackson behind him. "The mermen are coming through."

There seemed to be about six of them, boring holes through the doors and walls. Behind them, the doctor saw the silhouettes of mermaid spiders through the curtains, twitching for prey.

The chief didn't seem to notice they were in danger as the drills broke through. Nor did Cheryl, who continued speaking in her soft crazed voice.

"In that story, a mermaid princess fell in love with a human prince," Cheryl said. "But they could not be together, because she could not walk on land."

The doctor held his trident out as the heads of the drill fish poked through, spraying sawdust into the room.

"They grew up, separated from each other," Cheryl continued. "Yet always longed for each other from afar."

Blood leaked from her mouth as she smiled.

"Keep them from getting inside," the doctor yelled, ramming his trident through a hole at one of the mermen. The spinning drill only bounced the spear away.

"Then one day something magical happened," Cheryl said. "The mermaid princess transformed, growing legs so that she could walk on land and marry the human prince whom she loved. They lived happily ever after as husband and wife."

The doctor looked back to see the mermaid and the chief kissing, holding each other as the drill fish invaded the mansion. They didn't care about anything else. They were absorbed in each other. It really was as if they were lovers. The doctor didn't understand how it was possible. To him it made about as much sense as a goldfish falling in love with a snake.

"That's exactly what happened to my brother," Cheryl continued. "He's become a part of a real life fairy tale. A beautiful, wonderful fairy tale."

"Let's get out of here," the doctor said to Jackson. "There's too many of them. We'll be trapped."

Jackson didn't move. She stared at the dancing lovers, entranced by them.

"Forget about them," the doctor told her. "They're long gone. All of them. There's nothing we can do."

The doctor pulled Jackson toward the door, but she dragged her feet. She went limp. It didn't seem like she wanted to flee.

"Jackson, come on," the doctor said. "Let's go."

She didn't move.

"Jackson?" The doctor shook her. "What's wrong with you?"

She didn't say anything, just staring at him through the gasmask.

"Are you okay?" the doctor asked.

When he removed the gasmask, he fell back in horror. Her once cheerful child-like face had become infected with the food people disease. It overtook her even faster than with the boatman. He could see it spreading across her face like a swarm of bees crawling on a hive. The young woman was becoming nothing more than mindless human livestock.

Losing Jackson made Doctor Black cry. This was very surprising to the doctor. He had never cried before, not for anything. He did not even cry when he lost his wife or said goodbye to his daughter. Not even when faced with his own death. But seeing this girl reduced to such a fate—when she had so much to live for, had endured so much suffering during her short life—the doctor shed a tear. It was only one, but to Doctor Black one tear was a whole river. It gushed through the grooves Jackson had carved into his face, spiraling around his cheek like a marble in a funnel. The lone tear circled his chin and curved around his neck. It went through the spirals on his back and arms and legs until it traversed the course of his body.

And when he finally turned to leave her, he did not run toward the exit. He could care less if he escaped. There was no future waiting for him out that door. All he had was what was in front of him, in the present. All he had was his fury.

With his trident raised over his shoulder like a javelin, he charged the mermen, the precious endangered mermen, and stabbed them through their thin fishy skulls. He did not do it to defend himself or protect any of the surviving villagers. He only did it because at that moment he needed something to kill.

Fuck the mermen. They were all going to die.

By the time Endangered Species Security had arrived, the hillside was covered in the bodies of mermaids and mermen.

The sun was coming up. Doctor Black leaned against the doorway, the trident covered in fish blood, a cigarette burning in his mouth, the gasmask raised to the top of his forehead. There were still several fish creatures and rabid merchows running through the hills, but the doctor didn't attack them unless they got too close. He was busy attempting to enjoy the little time he had left of his life.

The ESS landed in two helicopters on the hill near the chief's mansion. Three agents stepped out and came toward him.

"Here come the freaks," the doctor said to himself.

He meant freaks quite literally. The agents of Endangered Species Security were not human. They were bioengineered monstrosities. They had the brains of men, but their bodies were a mashup of dozens of endangered species meshed together like surreal Frankenstein monsters. The point was to keep endangered species DNA alive while at the same time giving the agents more sympathy for the plight of the many animals facing extinction.

"What the hell happened here?" squawked one of the ESS agents, staring in horror at the mermaid corpses. "This is a bloodbath."

The agent was a mix of beluga sturgeon and hawksbill turtle with a bald eagle head. The other two agents were a mix of black rhino and golden seal with giant panda heads.

"Doctor Black," the head agent said as he approached. "Please explain why we've arrived to a massacre. Where is the village chief?"

The agent pushed past the doctor into the mansion, stomping through the entryway.

"The mermaids had to be put down," the doctor said.

He lit up another cigarette.

When the ESS agent saw the chief dancing with his mermaid wife, kissing and groping each other, he nearly threw up the pickled herring he had for breakfast.

"He's gone a little mad," the doctor said.

"He's gone mad?" cried Eagle Head. "He's gone mad! I think I'm the one who's going mad! Look around you." He pointed at the merman bodies surrounding them, but disregarded the dead humans cocooned in the spider web on the ceiling. "Look at all this carnage. Look at this insanity."

"Yeah, I've seen it," the doctor said, taking a drag from his cigarette.

The monstrous agent stomped at the doctor and plucked the cigarette out of his mouth with his eagle beak and then spit it aside.

"These are endangered species we're dealing with," cried Eagle Head. "How can you take their deaths so lightly?"

The doctor chuckled and turned away.

"You don't have to be so concerned about them," the doctor said.

He pointed through the window at the village below. The fog had cleared, revealing the bloodshed. Dozens of mermaids spider-walked down the beach, dragging the last of their human prey into the ocean. They were perfect, beautiful predators. Only a ghost town was left in their wake.

The doctor said, "As a species, the mermaids are going to do just fine from here on out."

Then he pointed inside of the mansion. The chief was licking his wife's fishy neck and grabbing at her pale green breasts. The younger sister, Amy, was staring blankly out into space, taking bites out of her food baby's legs and belly like a screaming spool of cotton candy. The older sister, Cheryl, was laughing with glee as her belly burst open and hundreds of baby mermaid spiders crawled out of the hollow cavity to eat her alive. And Jackson, now completely transformed by the infection, lay writhing on the ground, mindlessly fucking a surviving merman as he injected her full of poison and drilled a hole through the center of her face.

"It's the human species you'll have to worry about," the doctor said.

Then he lowered the gasmask over his face and walked out of the house, grabbing his trident on the porch and heading down the hill toward the village.

He didn't know if anyone was still alive down there, but while his heart was still capable of pumping blood through his grotesquely misshapen body he hoped he could save at least one of those sorry monochrome bastards from total extinction.

111

BONUS SECTION

This is the part of the book where we would have published an afterword by the author but he insisted on drawing a comic strip instead for reasons we don't quite understand.

I hope you enjoyed my new book *Village of the mermaids.*

It's me CM3!

Aren't mermaids awesome? I think mermaids are 10 times more awesome than dolphinmaids.

really passionate about mermaids

What's wrong with dolphinmaids?

dolphinmaid

Ummm... Nothing's wrong with dolphinmaids...

I like being a dolphinmaid...

sad

There's nothing wrong with any of you lovely lady fish creature things...
BANG!
BANG!
BANG!
BANG!
BANG!
dead

THE
END

ABOUT THE AUTHOR

Carlton Mellick III is one of the leading authors of the bizarro fiction subgenre. Since 2001, his books have drawn an international cult following, despite the fact that they have been shunned by most libraries and chain bookstores.

He won the Wonderland Book Award for his novel, *Warrior Wolf Women of the Wasteland*, in 2009. His short fiction has appeared in *Vice Magazine, The Year's Best Fantasy and Horror #16, The Magazine of Bizarro Fiction,* and *Zombies: Encounters with the Hungry Dead*, among others. He is also a graduate of Clarion West, where he studied under the likes of Chuck Palahniuk, Connie Willis, and Cory Doctorow.

He lives in Portland, OR, the bizarro fiction mecca.

Visit him online at **www.carltonmellick.com**

BIZARRO BOOKS

CATALOG   SPRING 2012

ERASERHEAD PRESS

Your major resource for the bizarro fiction genre:

WWW.BIZARROCENTRAL.COM

Introduce yourselves to the bizarro fiction genre and all of its authors with the Bizarro Starter Kit series. Each volume features short novels and short stories by ten of the leading bizarro authors, designed to give you a perfect sampling of the genre for only $10.

BB-0X1
"The Bizarro Starter Kit"
(Orange)
Featuring D. Harlan Wilson, Carlton Mellick III, Jeremy Robert Johnson, Kevin L Donihe, Gina Ranalli, Andre Duza, Vincent W. Sakowski, Steve Beard, John Edward Lawson, and Bruce Taylor.
236 pages $10

BB-0X2
"The Bizarro Starter Kit"
(Blue)
Featuring Ray Fracalossy, Jeremy C. Shipp, Jordan Krall, Mykle Hansen, Andersen Prunty, Eckhard Gerdes, Bradley Sands, Steve Aylett, Christian TeBordo, and Tony Rauch. **244 pages $10**

BB-0X2
"The Bizarro Starter Kit"
(Purple)
Featuring Russell Edson, Athena Villaverde, David Agranoff, Matthew Revert, Andrew Goldfarb, Jeff Burk, Garrett Cook, Kris Saknussemm, Cody Goodfellow, and Cameron Pierce **264 pages $10**

BB-001 **"The Kafka Effekt" D. Harlan Wilson** — A collection of forty-four irreal short stories loosely written in the vein of Franz Kafka, with more than a pinch of William S. Burroughs sprinkled on top. **211 pages $14**

BB-002 **"Satan Burger" Carlton Mellick III** — The cult novel that put Carlton Mellick III on the map ... Six punks get jobs at a fast food restaurant owned by the devil in a city violently overpopulated by surreal alien cultures. **236 pages $14**

BB-003 **"Some Things Are Better Left Unplugged" Vincent Sakwoski** — Join The Man and his Nemesis, the obese tabby, for a nightmare roller coaster ride into this postmodern fantasy. **152 pages $10**

BB-004 **"Shall We Gather At the Garden?" Kevin L Donihe** — Donihe's Debut novel. Midgets take over the world, The Church of Lionel Richie vs. The Church of the Byrds, plant porn and more! **244 pages $14**

BB-005 **"Razor Wire Pubic Hair" Carlton Mellick III** — A genderless humandildo is purchased by a razor dominatrix and brought into her nightmarish world of bizarre sex and mutilation. **176 pages $11**

BB-006 **"Stranger on the Loose" D. Harlan Wilson** — The fiction of Wilson's 2nd collection is planted in the soil of normalcy, but what grows out of that soil is a dark, witty, otherworldly jungle... **228 pages $14**

BB-007 **"The Baby Jesus Butt Plug" Carlton Mellick III** — Using clones of the Baby Jesus for anal sex will be the hip sex fetish of the future. **92 pages $10**

BB-008 **"Fishyfleshed" Carlton Mellick III** — The world of the past is an illogical flatland lacking in dimension and color, a sick-scape of crispy squid people wandering the desert for no apparent reason. **260 pages $14**

BB-009 **"Dead Bitch Army" Andre Duza** — Step into a world filled with racist teenagers, cannibals, 100 warped Uncle Sams, automobiles with razor-sharp teeth, living graffiti, and a pissed-off zombie bitch out for revenge. **344 pages $16**

BB-010 **"The Menstruating Mall" Carlton Mellick III** — "The Breakfast Club meets Chopping Mall as directed by David Lynch." - Brian Keene **212 pages $12**

BB-011 **"Angel Dust Apocalypse" Jeremy Robert Johnson** — Meth-heads, man-made monsters, and murderous Neo-Nazis. "Seriously amazing short stories..." - Chuck Palahniuk, author of Fight Club **184 pages $11**

BB-012 **"Ocean of Lard" Kevin L Donihe / Carlton Mellick III** — A parody of those old Choose Your Own Adventure kid's books about some very odd pirates sailing on a sea made of animal fat. **176 pages $12**

BB-015 **"Foop!" Chris Genoa** — Strange happenings are going on at Dactyl, Inc, the world's first and only time travel tourism company. "A surreal pie in the face!" - Christopher Moore **300 pages $14**

BB-020 **"Punk Land" Carlton Mellick III** — In the punk version of Heaven, the anarchist utopia is threatened by corporate fascism and only Goblin, Mortician's sperm, and a blue-mohawked female assassin named Shark Girl can stop them. **284 pages $15**

BB-027 **"Siren Promised" Jeremy Robert Johnson & Alan M Clark** — Nominated for the Bram Stoker Award. A potent mix of bad drugs, bad dreams, brutal bad guys, and surreal/incredible art by Alan M. Clark. **190 pages $13**

BB-031**"Sea of the Patchwork Cats" Carlton Mellick III** — A quiet dreamlike tale set in the ashes of the human race. For Mellick enthusiasts who also adore The Twilight Zone. **112 pages $10**

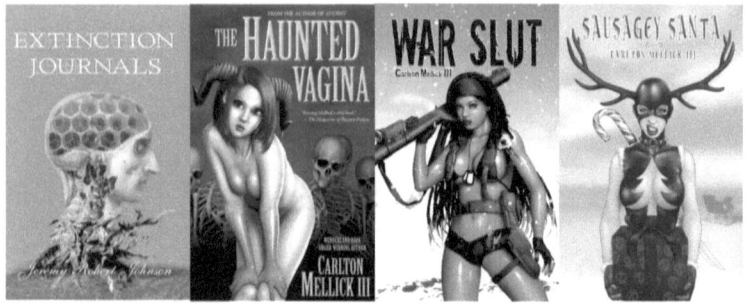

BB-032 **"Extinction Journals" Jeremy Robert Johnson** — An uncanny voyage across a newly nuclear America where one man must confront the problems associated with loneliness, insane dieties, radiation, love, and an ever-evolving cockroach suit with a mind of its own. **104 pages $10**

BB-037 **"The Haunted Vagina" Carlton Mellick III** — It's difficult to love a woman whose vagina is a gateway to the world of the dead. **132 pages $10**

BB-043 **"War Slut" Carlton Mellick III** — Part "1984," part "Waiting for Godot," and part action horror video game adaptation of John Carpenter's "The Thing." **116 pages $10**

BB-047 **"Sausagey Santa" Carlton Mellick III** — A bizarro Christmas tale featuring Santa as a piratey mutant with a body made of sausages. 124 pages $10

BB-048 **"Misadventures in a Thumbnail Universe" Vincent Sakowski** — Dive deep into the surreal and satirical realms of neo-classical Blender Fiction, filled with television shoes and flesh-filled skies. **120 pages $10**

BB-053 **"Ballad of a Slow Poisoner" Andrew Goldfarb** — Millford Mutterwurst sat down on a Tuesday to take his afternoon tea, and made the unpleasant discovery that his elbows were becoming flatter. **128 pages $10**

BB-055 **"Help! A Bear is Eating Me" Mykle Hansen** — The bizarro, heartwarming, magical tale of poor planning, hubris and severe blood loss... **150 pages $11**

BB-056 **"Piecemeal June" Jordan Krall** — A man falls in love with a living sex doll, but with love comes danger when her creator comes after her with crab-squid assassins. **90 pages $9**

BB-058 **"The Overwhelming Urge" Andersen Prunty** — A collection of bizarro tales by Andersen Prunty. **150 pages $11**

BB-059 **"Adolf in Wonderland" Carlton Mellick III** — A dreamlike adventure that takes a young descendant of Adolf Hitler's design and sends him down the rabbit hole into a world of imperfection and disorder. **180 pages $11**

BB-061 **"Ultra Fuckers" Carlton Mellick III** — Absurdist suburban horror about a couple who enter an upper middle class gated community but can't find their way out. **108 pages $9**

BB-062 **"House of Houses" Kevin L. Donihe** — An odd man wants to marry his house. Unfortunately, all of the houses in the world collapse at the same time in the Great House Holocaust. Now he must travel to House Heaven to find his departed fiancee. **172 pages $11**

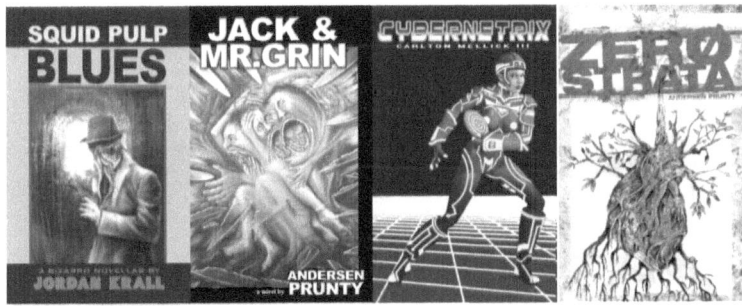

BB-064 **"Squid Pulp Blues" Jordan Krall** — In these three bizarro-noir novellas, the reader is thrown into a world of murderers, drugs made from squid parts, deformed gun-toting veterans, and a mischievous apocalyptic donkey. **204 pages $12**

BB-065 **"Jack and Mr. Grin" Andersen Prunty** — "When Mr. Grin calls you can hear a smile in his voice. Not a warm and friendly smile, but the kind that seizes your spine in fear. You don't need to pay your phone bill to hear it. That smile is in every line of Prunty's prose." - Tom Bradley. **208 pages $12**

BB-066 **"Cybernetrix" Carlton Mellick III** — What would you do if your normal everyday world was slowly mutating into the video game world from Tron? **212 pages $12**

BB-072 **"Zerostrata" Andersen Prunty** — Hansel Nothing lives in a tree house, suffers from memory loss, has a very eccentric family, and falls in love with a woman who runs naked through the woods every night. **144 pages $11**

BB-073 **"The Egg Man" Carlton Mellick III** — It is a world where humans reproduce like insects. Children are the property of corporations, and having an enormous ten-foot brain implanted into your skull is a grotesque sexual fetish. Mellick's industrial urban dystopia is one of his darkest and grittiest to date. **184 pages $11**

BB-074 **"Shark Hunting in Paradise Garden" Cameron Pierce** — A group of strange humanoid religious fanatics travel back in time to the Garden of Eden to discover it is invested with hundreds of giant flying maneating sharks. **150 pages $10**

BB-075 **"Apeshit" Carlton Mellick III** - Friday the 13th meets Visitor Q. Six hipster teens go to a cabin in the woods inhabited by a deformed killer. An incredibly fucked-up parody of B-horror movies with a bizarro slant. **192 pages $12**

BB-076 **"Fuckers of Everything on the Crazy Shitting Planet of the Vomit At msosphere" Mykle Hansen** - Three bizarro satires. Monster Cocks, Journey to the Center of Agnes Cuddlebottom, and Crazy Shitting Planet. **228 pages $12**

BB-077 **"The Kissing Bug" Daniel Scott Buck** — In the tradition of Roald Dahl, Tim Burton, and Edward Gorey, comes this bizarro anti-war children's story about a bohemian conenose kissing bug who falls in love with a human woman. **116 pages $10**

BB-078 **"MachoPoni" Lotus Rose** — It's My Little Pony... *Bizarro* style! A long time ago Poniworld was split in two. On one side of the Jagged Line is the Pastel Kingdom, a magical land of music, parties, and positivity. On the other side of the Jagged Line is Dark Kingdom inhabited by an army of undead ponies. **148 pages $11**

BB-079 **"The Faggiest Vampire" Carlton Mellick III** — A Roald Dahl-esque children's story about two faggy vampires who partake in a mustache competition to find out which one is truly the faggiest. **104 pages $10**

BB-080 **"Sky Tongues" Gina Ranalli** — The autobiography of Sky Tongues, the biracial hermaphrodite actress with tongues for fingers. Follow her strange life story as she rises from freak to fame. **204 pages $12**

BB-081 **"Washer Mouth" Kevin L. Donihe** - A washing machine becomes human and pursues his dream of meeting his favorite soap opera star. **244 pages $11**

BB-082 **"Shatnerquake" Jeff Burk** - All of the characters ever played by William Shatner are suddenly sucked into our world. Their mission: hunt down and destroy the real William Shatner. **100 pages $10**

BB-083 **"The Cannibals of Candyland" Carlton Mellick III** - There exists a race of cannibals that are made of candy. They live in an underground world made out of candy. One man has dedicated his life to killing them all. **170 pages $11**

BB-084 **"Slub Glub in the Weird World of the Weeping Willows"** **Andrew Goldfarb** - The charming tale of a blue glob named Slub Glub who helps the weeping willows whose tears are flooding the earth. There are also hyenas, ghosts, and a voodoo priest **100 pages $10**

BB-085 **"Super Fetus" Adam Pepper** - Try to abort this fetus and he'll kick your ass! **104 pages $10**

BB-086 **"Fistful of Feet" Jordan Krall** - A bizarro tribute to spaghetti westerns, featuring Cthulhu-worshipping Indians, a woman with four feet, a crazed gunman who is obsessed with sucking on candy, Syphilis-ridden mutants, sexually transmitted tattoos, and a house devoted to the freakiest fetishes. **228 pages $12**

BB-087 **"Ass Goblins of Auschwitz" Cameron Pierce** - It's Monty Python meets Nazi exploitation in a surreal nightmare as can only be imagined by Bizarro author Cameron Pierce. **104 pages $10**

BB-088 **"Silent Weapons for Quiet Wars" Cody Goodfellow** - "This is high-end psychological surrealist horror meets bottom-feeding low-life crime in a techno-thrilling science fiction world full of Lovecraft and magic..." -John Skipp **212 pages $12**

BB-089 **"Warrior Wolf Women of the Wasteland" Carlton Mellick III**
— Road Warrior Werewolves versus McDonaldland Mutants...post-apocalyptic fiction has never been quite like this. **316 pages $13**

BB-091 **"Super Giant Monster Time" Jeff Burk** — A tribute to choose your own adventures and Godzilla movies. Will you escape the giant monsters that are rampaging the fuck out of your city and shit? Or will you join the mob of alien-controlled punk rockers causing chaos in the streets? What happens next depends on you. **188 pages $12**

BB-092 **"Perfect Union" Cody Goodfellow** — "Cronenberg's THE FLY on a grand scale: human/insect gene-spliced body horror, where the human hive politics are as shocking as the gore." -John Skipp. **272 pages $13**

BB-093 **"Sunset with a Beard" Carlton Mellick III** — 14 stories of surreal science fiction. **200 pages $12**

BB-094 **"My Fake War" Andersen Prunty** — The absurd tale of an unlikely soldier forced to fight a war that, quite possibly, does not exist. It's Rambo meets Waiting for Godot in this subversive satire of American values and the scope of the human imagination. **128 pages $11**

BB-095 **"Lost in Cat Brain Land" Cameron Pierce** — Sad stories from a surreal world. A fascist mustache, the ghost of Franz Kafka, a desert inside a dead cat. Primordial entities mourn the death of their child. The desperate serve tea to mysterious creatures. A hopeless romantic falls in love with a pterodactyl. And much more. **152 pages $11**

BB-096 **"The Kobold Wizard's Dildo of Enlightenment +2" Carlton Mellick III** — A Dungeons and Dragons parody about a group of people who learn they are only made up characters in an AD&D campaign and must find a way to resist their nerdy teenaged players and retarded dungeon master in order to survive. 232 **pages $12**

BB-098 **"A Hundred Horrible Sorrows of Ogner Stump" Andrew Goldfarb** — Goldfarb's acclaimed comic series. A magical and weird journey into the horrors of everyday life. **164 pages $11**

BB-099 **"Pickled Apocalypse of Pancake Island" Cameron Pierce**—A demented fairy tale about a pickle, a pancake, and the apocalypse. **102 pages $8**

BB-100 **"Slag Attack" Andersen Prunty**— Slag Attack features four visceral, noir stories about the living, crawling apocalypse. A slag is what survivors are calling the slug-like maggots raining from the sky, burrowing inside people, and hollowing out their flesh and their sanity. **148 pages $11**

BB-101 **"Slaughterhouse High" Robert Devereaux**—A place where schools are built with secret passageways, rebellious teens get zippers installed in their mouths and genitals, and once a year, on that special night, one couple is slaughtered and the bits of their bodies are kept as souvenirs. **304 pages $13**

BB-102 **"The Emerald Burrito of Oz" John Skipp & Marc Levinthal** —OZ IS REAL! Magic is real! The gate is really in Kansas! And America is finally allowing Earth tourists to visit this weird-ass, mysterious land. But when Gene of Los Angeles heads off for summer vacation in the Emerald City, little does he know that a war is brewing...a war that could destroy both worlds. **280 pages $13**

BB-103 **"The Vegan Revolution... with Zombies" David Agranoff** — When there's no more meat in hell, the vegans will walk the earth. **160 pages $11**

BB-104 **"The Flappy Parts" Kevin L Donihe**—Poems about bunnies, LSD, and police abuse. You know, things that matter. 132 **pages $11**

BB-105 **"Sorry I Ruined Your Orgy" Bradley Sands**—Bizarro humorist Bradley Sands returns with one of the strangest, most hilarious collections of the year. **130 pages $11**

BB-106 **"Mr. Magic Realism" Bruce Taylor**—Like Golden Age science fiction comics written by Freud, *Mr. Magic Realism* is a strange, insightful adventure that spans the furthest reaches of the galaxy, exploring the hidden caverns in the hearts and minds of men, women, aliens, and biomechanical cats. **152 pages $11**

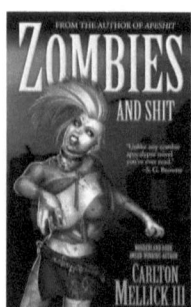   

BB-107 **"Zombies and Shit" Carlton Mellick III**—"Battle Royale" meets "Return of the Living Dead." Mellick's bizarro tribute to the zombie genre. **308 pages $13**

BB-108 **"The Cannibal's Guide to Ethical Living" Mykle Hansen**— Over a five star French meal of fine wine, organic vegetables and human flesh, a lunatic delivers a witty, chilling, disturbingly sane argument in favor of eating the rich.. **184 pages $11**

BB-109 **"Starfish Girl" Athena Villaverde**—In a post-apocalyptic underwater dome society, a girl with a starfish growing from her head and an assassin with sea anenome hair are on the run from a gang of mutant fish men. **160 pages $11**

BB-110 **"Lick Your Neighbor" Chris Genoa**—Mutant ninjas, a talking whale, kung fu masters, maniacal pilgrims, and an alcoholic clown populate Chris Genoa's surreal, darkly comical and unnerving reimagining of the first Thanksgiving. **303 pages $13**

BB-111 **"Night of the Assholes" Kevin L. Donihe**—A plague of assholes is infecting the countryside. Normal everyday people are transforming into jerks, snobs, dicks, and douchebags. And they all have only one purpose: to make your life a living hell.. **192 pages $11**

BB-112 **"Jimmy Plush, Teddy Bear Detective" Garrett Cook**—Hardboiled cases of a private detective trapped within a teddy bear body. **180 pages $11**

BB-113 **"The Deadheart Shelters" Forrest Armstrong**—The hip hop lovechild of William Burroughs and Dali... **144 pages $11**

BB-114 **"Eyeballs Growing All Over Me... Again" Tony Raugh**— Absurd, surreal, playful, dream-like, whimsical, and a lot of fun to read. **144 pages $11**

BB-115 **"Whargoul" Dave Brockie** — From the killing grounds of Stalingrad to the death camps of the holocaust. From torture chambers in Iraq to race riots in the United States, the Whargoul was there, killing and raping. **244 pages $12**

BB-116 **"By the Time We Leave Here, We'll Be Friends" J. David Osborne** — A David Lynchian nightmare set in a Russian gulag, where its prisoners, guards, traitors, soldiers, lovers, and demons fight for survival and their own rapidly deteriorating humanity. **168 pages $11**

BB-117 **"Christmas on Crack" edited by Carlton Mellick III** — Perverted Christmas Tales for the whole family! . . . as long as every member of your family is over the age of 18. **168 pages $11**

BB-118 **"Crab Town" Carlton Mellick III** — Radiation fetishists, balloon people, mutant crabs, sail-bike road warriors, and a love affair between a woman and an H-Bomb. This is one mean asshole of a city. Welcome to Crab Town. **100 pages $8**

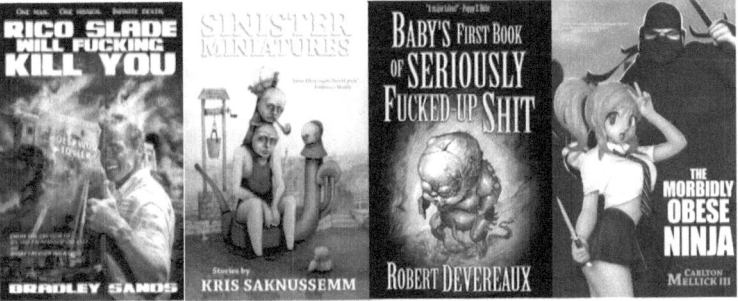

BB-119 **"Rico Slade Will Fucking Kill You" Bradley Sands** — Rico Slade is an action hero. Rico Slade can rip out a throat with his bare hands. Rico Slade's favorite food is the honey-roasted peanut. Rico Slade will fucking kill everyone. A novel. **122 pages $8**

BB-120 **"Sinister Miniatures" Kris Saknussemm** — The definitive collection of short fiction by Kris Saknussemm, confirming that he is one of the best, most daring writers of the weird to emerge in the twenty-first century. **180 pages $11**

BB-121 **"Baby's First Book of Seriously Fucked up Shit" Robert Devereaux** — Ten stories of the strange, the gross, and the just plain fucked up from one of the most original voices in horror. **176 pages $11**

BB-122 **"The Morbidly Obese Ninja" Carlton Mellick III** — These days, if you want to run a successful company . . . you're going to need a lot of ninjas. **92 pages $8**

BB-123 **"Abortion Arcade" Cameron Pierce** — An intoxicating blend of body horror and midnight movie madness, reminiscent of early David Lynch and the splatterpunks at their most sublime. **172 pages $11**

BB-124 **"Black Hole Blues" Patrick Wensink** — A hilarious double helix of country music and physics. **196 pages $11**

BB-125 **"Barbarian Beast Bitches of the Badlands" Carlton Mellick III** — Three prequels and sequels to *Warrior Wolf Women of the Wasteland*. **284 pages $13**

BB-126 **"The Traveling Dildo Salesman" Kevin L. Donihe** — A nightmare comedy about destiny, faith, and sex toys. Also featuring Donihe's most lurid and infamous short stories: *Milky Agitation, Two-Way Santa, The Helen Mower, Living Room Zombies*, and *Revenge of the Living Masturbation Rag.* **108 pages $8**

BB-127 **"Metamorphosis Blues" Bruce Taylor** — Enter a land of love beasts, intergalactic cowboys, and rock 'n roll. A land where Sears Catalogs are doorways to insanity and men keep mysterious black boxes. Welcome to the monstrous mind of Mr. Magic Realism. **136 pages $11**

BB-128 **"The Driver's Guide to Hitting Pedestrians" Andersen Prunty** — A pocket guide to the twenty-three most painful things in life, written by the most well-adjusted man in the universe. **108 pages $8**

BB-129 **"Island of the Super People" Kevin Shamel** — Four students and their anthropology professor journey to a remote island to study its indigenous population. But this is no ordinary native culture. They're super heroes and villains with flesh costumes and outlandish abilities like self-detonation, musical eyelashes, and microwave hands. **194 pages $11**

BB-130 **"Fantastic Orgy" Carlton Mellick III** — Shark Sex, mutant cats, and strange sexually transmitted diseases. Featuring the stories: *Candy-coated, Ear Cat, Fantastic Orgy, City Hobgoblins*, and *Porno in August.* **136 pages $9**

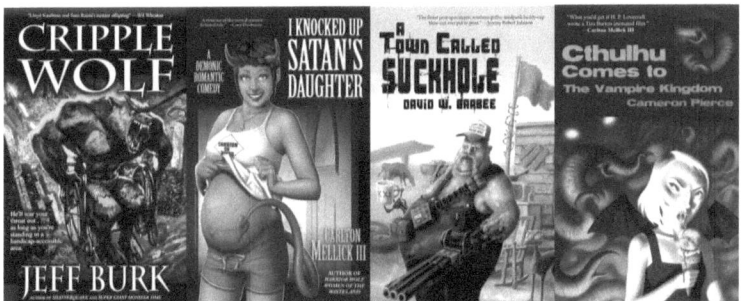

BB-131 **"Cripple Wolf" Jeff Burk** — Part man. Part wolf. 100% crippled. Also including *Punk Rock Nursing Home, Adrift with Space Badgers, Cook for Your Life, Just Another Day in the Park, Frosty and the Full Monty*, and *House of Cats*. **152 pages $10**

BB-132 **"I Knocked Up Satan's Daughter" Carlton Mellick III** — An adorable, violent, fantastical love story. A romantic comedy for the bizarro fiction reader. **152 pages $10**

BB-133 **"A Town Called Suckhole" David W. Barbee** — Far into the future, in the nuclear bowels of post-apocalyptic Dixie, there is a town. A town of derelict mobile homes, ancient junk, and mutant wildlife. A town of slack jawed rednecks who bask in the splendors of moonshine and mud boggin'. A town dedicated to the bloody and demented legacy of the Old South. A town called Suckhole. **144 pages $10**

BB-134 **"Cthulhu Comes to the Vampire Kingdom" Cameron Pierce** — What you'd get if H. P. Lovecraft wrote a Tim Burton animated film. **148 pages $11**

BB-135 **"I am Genghis Cum" Violet LeVoit** — From the savage Arctic tundra to post-partum mutations to your missing daughter's unmarked grave, join visionary madwoman Violet LeVoit in this non-stop eight-story onslaught of full-tilt Bizarro punk lit thrills. **124 pages $9**

BB-136 **"Haunt" Laura Lee Bahr** — A tripping-balls Los Angeles noir, where a mysterious dame drags you through a time-warping Bizarro hall of mirrors. **316 pages $13**

BB-137 **"Amazing Stories of the Flying Spaghetti Monster" edited by Cameron Pierce** — Like an all-spaghetti evening of Adult Swim, the Flying Spaghetti Monster will show you the many realms of His Noodly Appendage. Learn of those who worship him and the lives he touches in distant, mysterious ways. **228 pages $12**

BB-138 **"Wave of Mutilation" Douglas Lain** — A dream-pop exploration of modern architecture and the American identity, *Wave of Mutilation* is a Zen finger trap for the 21st century. **100 pages $8**

BB-139 **"Hooray for Death!" Mykle Hansen** — Famous Author Mykle Hansen draws unconventional humor from deaths tiny and large, and invites you to laugh while you can. **128 pages $10**

BB-140 **"Hypno-hog's Moonshine Monster Jamboree" Andrew Goldfarb** — Hicks, Hogs, Horror! Goldfarb is back with another strange illustrated tale of backwoods weirdness. **120 pages $9**

BB-141 **"Broken Piano For President" Patrick Wensink** — A comic masterpiece about the fast food industry, booze, and the necessity to choose happiness over work and security. **372 pages $15**

BB-142 **"Please Do Not Shoot Me in the Face" Bradley Sands** — A novel in three parts, *Please Do Not Shoot Me in the Face: A Novel*, is the story of one boy detective, the worst ninja in the world, and the great American fast food wars. It is a novel of loss, destruction, and--incredibly--genuine hope. **224 pages $12**

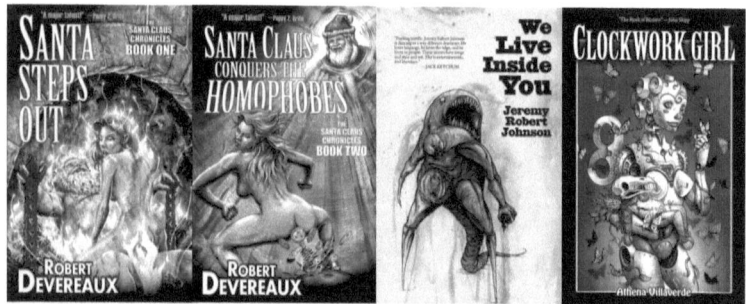

BB-143 **"Santa Steps Out" Robert Devereaux** — Sex, Death, and Santa Claus ... The ultimate erotic Christmas story is back. **294 pages $13**

BB-144 **"Santa Conquers the Homophobes" Robert Devereaux** — "I wish I could hope to ever attain one-thousandth the perversity of Robert Devereaux's toenail clippings." - Poppy Z. Brite **316 pages $13**

BB-145 **"We Live Inside You" Jeremy Robert Johnson** — "Jeremy Robert Johnson is dancing to a way different drummer. He loves language, he loves the edge, and he loves us people. These stories have range and style and wit. This is entertainment... and literature."- Jack Ketchum **188 pages $11**

BB-146 **"Clockwork Girl" Athena Villaverde** — Urban fairy tales for the weird girl in all of us. Like a combination of Francesca Lia Block, Charles de Lint, Kathe Koja, Tim Burton, and Hayao Miyazaki, her stories are cute, kinky, edgy, magical, provocative, and strange, full of poetic imagery and vicious sexuality. **160 pages $10**

BB-147 "Armadillo Fists" Carlton Mellick III — A weird-as-hell gangster story set in a world where people drive giant mechanical dinosaurs instead of cars. **168 pages $11**

BB-148 "Gargoyle Girls of Spider Island" Cameron Pierce — Four college seniors venture out into open waters for the tropical party weekend of a lifetime. Instead of a teenage sex fantasy, they find themselves in a nightmare of pirates, sharks, and sex-crazed monsters. **100 pages $8**

BB-149 "The Handsome Squirm" by Carlton Mellick III — Like Franz Kafka's *The Trial* meets an erotic body horror version of *The Blob*. **158 pages $11**

BB-150 "Tentacle Death Trip" Jordan Krall — It's *Death Race 2000* meets H. P. Lovecraft in bizarro author Jordan Krall's best and most suspenseful work to date. **224 pages $12**

BB-151 "The Obese" Nick Antosca — Like Alfred Hitchcock's *The Birds*... but with obese people. **108 pages $10**

BB-152 "All-Monster Action!" Cody Goodfellow — The world gave him a blank check and a demand: Create giant monsters to fight our wars. But Dr. Otaku was not satisfied with mere chaos and mass destruction.... **216 pages $12**

BB-153 "Ugly Heaven" Carlton Mellick III — Heaven is no longer a paradise. It was once a blissful utopia full of wonders far beyond human comprehension. But the afterlife is now in ruins. It has become an ugly, lonely wasteland populated by strange monstrous beasts, masturbating angels, and sad man-like beings wallowing in the remains of the once-great Kingdom of God. **106 pages $8**

BB-154 "Space Walrus" Kevin L. Donihe — Walter is supposed to go where no walrus has ever gone before, but all this astronaut walrus really wants is to take it easy on the intense training, escape the chimpanzee bullies, and win the love of his human trainer Dr. Stephanie. **160 pages $11**